MARYLAND: GHOST HARBOR

Anne put her hand to her chest and tried to slow the beating of her heart. And then she said, "No." She frowned and stamped her foot. This was crazy. This wasn't real. The man after her was not real; this outhouse wasn't real. It couldn't be. She must have slipped on a slick spot on the aquarium floor, fallen and hit her head. She was certainly unconscious or dreaming, and the only way to stop it was to take control of her own nightmare. The only way to stop it was to confront it and deny any of it was true.

Tossing back her head, Anne unlatched the outhouse door, stepped outside, and cried, "None of this is real. I demand that it stop, and I command myself to wake up! Now!"

She closed her eyes, knowing that when she opened them she would be back with her school friends.

She opened her eyes. Staring back at her were the red, wild eyes of the man with the sword and filthy shirt. He grinned, his lower lip cracking and oozing blood.

"You silly pig," he said, as he yanked a length of rope from his waistband and grabbed Anne's hands in order to tie them together.

AMERICAN Chills

MARYLAND:
Ghost Harbor

Elizabeth Massie

Z·FAVE
KENSINGTON PUBLISHING CORP.

Z*FAVE BOOKS are published by

Kensington Publishing Corp.
850 Third Avenue
New York, NY 10022

First Printing: September, 1995

Printed in the United States of America

For Elizabeth Jennings Lawson,
with much love.

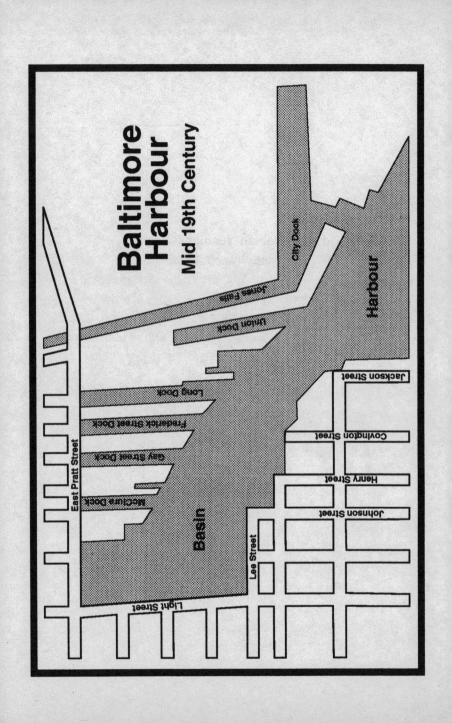

Baltimore
Harbour
Mid 19th Century

City Dock

Jones Falls

Union Dock

Harbour

Jackson Street

Long Dock

Frederick Street Dock

Covington Street

Gay Street Dock

East Pratt Street

Henry Street

McClure Dock

Johnson Street

Basin

Lee Street

Light Street

Introduction

Maryland, an important industrial and shipping state, lies in the northeast corner of the Southern states. The state was named for Queen Henrietta Maria, wife of King Charles I of England. In the early and middle 1800s, Baltimore became a leading seaport and a major shipbuilding center. Goods such as flour, wheat, and tobacco were moved by clipper ships from Baltimore's Inner Harbor to other states along the coast as well as to South American and European countries.

A northernmost slave state before the Civil War, Maryland sat on the border between slavery and freedom. It was the last piece of land some runaway slaves from the South had to cross before they found freedom in Pennsylvania, other northern free states, or Canada. Several routes of the Underground Railroad crossed through Maryland. At night, the runaways followed rivers and watched the sky for the "Drinking Gourd" (the Big Dipper) to show the way. During the day they hid in the forests or in homes of people who believed slavery was wrong. Some slaves, who didn't follow the Underground Railroad routes, tried to make their escape alone.

If the runaways made it to freedom, there was a reason to celebrate. But if the runaways were caught by the slave catchers, they were bound and returned to their often cruel masters in the South. Many were taken back on foot. Some, however, were transported on boats.

One

Her lungs hurt, but she kept on running. The woods were deep, dense, and dark, but her arms worked before her, pushing briars and branches out of the way. Her bare feet dug into the pebbles and moss, moving her onward.

He was behind her, and getting closer.

Millie knew her wrist was broken; each time she swung it forward, she could feel the screaming of cracked bone. Her head pounded, but she ran. She had no choice. Up through the forest she went, heading in the direction of the North Star. How far it was until safety, she couldn't know. But if she went any other way, it would be suicide. That she *did* know.

There were dogs with the man who chased her. They howled long, eerie songs that made Millie's blood chill. Dogs could follow her easily, and the man with them was strong and quick.

But she ran on.

Through the pounding of her head she tried to remember one of her mother's songs. She gritted her teeth as her broken wrist smacked into the side of a small tree and her bare feet came down on sharp-edged rocks. And she forced her mind to sing.

"Freedom, freedom, my baby,
Freedom, freedom, my baby,
Gonna have my freedom and the sun gonna shine
Freedom is the daylight
Lord, I'm gonna be fine."

The dogs were louder. They were gaining on her. They had more energy than she did. She had been traveling and hiding for weeks now, with little time to sleep or eat. And now they were after her. Millie's shin struck the top of a log as she tried to hurdle it, and she went down on her face.

"Oh, God help me," she whispered.

She scrambled upward. There was pine silt in her mouth. Her heart hammered in her throat.

The land sloped downward. Millie could hear rushing waters of a nearby river. *Yes,* she thought. Many rivers she had crossed in the last days had flowed northward. If she could get into the river and move along the edge, the dogs would lose her scent and the pain in her wrist would ease.

There was a crack of gunfire.

Millie shivered violently and ran down the knoll toward the sound of the river.

A man shouted, "Stop, you little pig! You know who I am!"

The ground was damper now, and covered with long, sleek grass which made it hard to keep her balance.

The dogs were very close now, perhaps only thirty yards back, and Millie bent over to run faster.

But then her feet hit a slick spot of grass and she slipped and tumbled down the hillside. Her wrist twisted backward as she rolled over it.

The pain made her scream.

The man behind her laughed.

She pulled her wrist into her body and tried to stand. She couldn't. The world was rolling, and her head spun. Finally, she managed to get on her feet, but her back remained bent. Her feet shuffled ahead, moving her to the river. The rushing was loud now; the river was, indeed, moving northward.

" 'Freedom is the daylight,' " she said, her voice distorted with tears. " 'Lord, I'm gonna be fine.' "

She could hear the man on the slope behind her, sliding down the wet grass, grunting with his footfalls. Between the dogs' barks, she heard their chains jingle.

A few more feet. Her bare toes scrambled, pushing her forward.

"Lord, I'm gonna be fine," she prayed.

And then there was a gun barrel jammed between her shoulders. A booted foot came down on her back. Millie lost her breath with the blow and fell flat. She gasped, trying to get air, and stared at the rushing waters of the river.

The man roughly rolled her over and grinned at her.

The two dogs stood by, their jobs done, sniffing at their master's legs.

"Good thing I got you 'fore you got in that water," the man said. He was ugly, his teeth rotted stubs, his forehead puckered with a long scar, his mouth and cheeks twisted in hate. There was a long sword in a sheath hanging from his belt. "You know me, girl," he said. "I'm Randolph Ritchie. Best slave catcher in all of Maryland."

Millie closed her eyes. If only it was a dream, she might wake from this. But the gun barrel jammed into her ribs, and her eyes flew open again.

The man leaned over her. Tobacco-stained spit dropped from his lip to her cheek. "I'm Randolph Ritchie. I don't never lose a runaway. I'll kill 'em before I do. If you got in the water, I'd have shot you dead." He stood straight and let out a loud laugh.

The dogs wagged their tails and sniffed Millie's side.

"Get up now, little pig," said Ritchie. "Got a boat waiting to take you home."

Two

"It's the cutest thing I've ever seen!"

"It's ugly. You need glasses."

"Do not," said Julie Sawyers, as she pressed her face to the glass of the marine tank. "Just look. It's kind of like a sea horse, only bigger and cuter. See how it hides in the seaweed? I want one for a pet."

"You want *everything* for a pet," said Anne Ferguson. "You wanted the manta ray for a pet. You wanted the hammerhead *shark* for a pet."

Julie turned her face from the glass and grinned. She was a pretty girl, with dark brown skin and short black hair. At thirteen, she was already five-feet-nine-inches tall. She stuck out her tongue at Anne. "So what? I like animals. Besides, we have a big enough bathtub to hold the manta ray *and* the shark."

Anne, a freckled girl a head shorter than Julie, flipped back a long strand of red hair and rolled her eyes. "I know you want to be a biologist when you grow up. But I can't see stepping into my bathtub and having one of those things wrap its little spiny tail around my leg. What *is* it, anyway?" She looked at the sign beneath the tank. "Hmmm. A Weedy Sea Dragon. I should have known it would have a weird name."

"*I* think it's cool."

"You know," said Anne thoughtfully, "you get a pet like that, and all the boys will want to come over to see it."

Julie made a face. "There aren't a whole lot of boys in our eighth grade class I *want* coming over to my house," she said.

"Except one or two," Anne challenged.

Julie looked around to make sure no one was listening, then nodded in agreement. "Except one or two."

"So where *is* Jerry now?" asked Anne.

Julie shrugged. Jerry, the cutest boy at Braunbeck Middle School, was somewhere in the aquarium, walking around with his friends John and Tim. Although Jerry was very popular, he wasn't stuck up. This was one reason Julie liked him. Also, he wasn't going with anyone at the moment. This was another reason Julie liked him. She hoped that if she and Anne walked slowly enough around the aquarium displays, they might run into the boys.

The students of Braunbeck Middle were on a full-day field trip at Baltimore's Inner Harbor. They had taken a boat ride, toured the shops of Harborplace, and now were spending the afternoon at the National Aquarium on the harbor shore. Everyone had gone at his or her own pace; some stayed a long time at the beluga whale pool on the first floor; some hurried ahead to visit the deep-sea display; some enjoyed the smaller tanks full of orange and red sea anemones and brightly striped schools of fish.

Julie and Anne moved away from the Weedy Sea Dragon and on to the next tank. Here, starfish with slender legs hugged mottled rocks and blue crabs scoured the sand for tidbits.

"I think I really am going to set up an aquarium at home," said Julie. "Maybe not with sharks or manta rays yet, but I bet I could make a pretty cool saltwater tank."

Anne laughed. "Then you better get a part-time job. That's an expensive hobby. When I wanted to buy a ten-gallon aquarium for some mollies last summer, it took me a month of baby-sitting to pay for everything I needed."

"So how much do you get for baby-sitting?"

Anne crossed her arms. "Two dollars an hour."

Julie wrinkled her nose. That was ridiculous, she thought. Two dollars an hour wasn't even minimum wage! "I'd *never* work for two dollars an hour. That's unfair. And isn't it illegal? That's like being a slave. My services are worth a *lot* more than that."

"But I baby-sit for my little cousin," Anne answered. "I do it because she's family, and my aunt can't afford much more."

"Well," said Julie, slowly. Suddenly, she felt a little bad, as though she'd judged Anne before hearing her whole story. She changed the subject. "What time is it?"

Anne pulled up the sleeve of her sweater and glanced

at her watch. "Almost four-thirty. We only have an hour until we have to leave."

"And," said Julie, "we haven't even seen the puffins yet!"

Suddenly, Anne turned and ran over to the balcony railing. She peered down at the first floor. "I thought so!" she said, turning back to Julie. "I heard Jerry and John. They're heading for the escalator. They'll be up here in a minute." She ran back to Julie, her red hair bouncing.

"And *you're* going to look like you've been waiting for them," said Julie. "Just calm down, girl."

Anne grinned. Julie and Anne turned their attention to the next tank. In it, a long, black, snakelike animal swam alone among thick seaweed. The sign beneath it read "Electric Eel."

"Are you going to get one of those, too?" Anne asked Julie. "It's not the kind of pet you can actually *pet,* is it?"

"No," said Julie. "But I like it. It's really different. Look at its eyes. It looks like it's saying, 'Hey, I have something really shocking to tell you. Come closer, come *real* close.' "

Anne pulled her friend's arm. "Duh. Glad you're going to be a biologist and not a comedian." She looked behind her to see if the boys had come up the escalator.

"Listen to what it says here." Julie put her finger to the printed description beneath the name sign. " 'The electric eel lives in the muddy rivers of South America. It can produce impulses of 200 to 300 volts. This is enough to stun a person or power a small motor.' That's really cool! Don't you think so, Anne?"

Anne didn't answer. Julie turned to ask her again. Anne was not there.

Julie frowned and looked around but didn't see her friend. *Strange,* Julie thought. *How could Anne have gone to another display out of view that quickly?*

Or, that quietly?

Julie walked to the end of the display hall and looked down the escalator. Maybe Anne had gone downstairs to see what was taking Jerry so long to come up. But Anne wasn't on the escalator. Jerry, John, and Tim, however, were on their way up.

Julie looked back down the hall to the electric eel tank. Anne was nowhere in sight. What was Anne trying to do? Play a trick? But that wasn't like her. Besides, Anne knew they all had to leave the aquarium in less than an hour.

Jerry reached the top of the escalator. He was wearing jeans and a long-sleeved blue shirt and he carried a bag from the aquarium gift shop.

Julie, usually too shy to speak to him, made herself talk. "Hey, Jerry, have you seen Anne?"

John and Tim got off behind Jerry. "No, why?" he asked. Then he laughed, a laugh that made his eyes crinkle up in such a cute way. "Is she lost or something?"

Julie smiled though she felt awkward. It was Jerry's laugh that made her feel so shy around him. "I think so. She was here just a second ago."

"Maybe she fell in the shark tank," said John. Unlike Jerry, John was a major jerk.

"No," Julie said. "But if you see her, tell her I'm looking for her, okay?" *And you can ask me to walk around with you, Jerry, if you want to,* she added silently.

But Jerry only said, "Okay, if I see her I'll tell her." And he walked off with Tim and John.

Julie crossed her arms. What was she supposed to do now? Stand around and wait for Anne to come back from wherever she was hiding? Try to join up with the boys and hope they didn't mind? Or view the rest of the aquarium alone?

"Anne!" Julie called, in no particular direction.

Anne didn't answer, and the two older women getting off the up escalator gave Julie a funny look.

Three

There was sand and dirt in her mouth, and she twisted her head up and away so she could catch her breath. What had happened? Had she tripped over something? She didn't remember the floor of the aquarium being so dirty. Or so cold.

She opened her eyes.

Gasping, Anne sat upright and looked around. She was not in the aquarium.

"Julie?" she called softly.

There was no answer.

Anne's head ached, and she rubbed her temple. Where *was* she? This place did not look familiar. She sat on the muddy, rocky ground on the shore of a harbor. The sun was behind her; it seemed to rest on top of the trees of the western woods. On the water were strange-looking boats, old-fashioned ships with sails and crates piled high on their decks. Rough wooden piers led out over the water, and gangplanks led from the piers to the decks of the ships. Behind her, unpainted wooden buildings sat, with mud paths between them. Littering the ground between the buildings and the water were stacks of crates and barrels with the words "England" and "France" stenciled on the sides, obviously waiting to be loaded onto the boats.

A mud-colored frog hopped up to Anne, stared at her with its unblinking eyes, then hopped away. Anne shook her head, closed her eyes tightly, then opened them again. The scene had not changed. She was still outside in the cold, on a shore she did not know.

Slowly, she stood up. She brushed some of the loose dirt from her jeans, but the mud streaked, leaving long stains. There had to be some reasonable explanation for what had happened to her. Whatever that was, maybe she was dreaming.

"This is crazy," she said sternly to herself. But her heart fluttered in fear.

She looked around at the closest building. It was a two-story construction of dark wood and few windows. She could hear singing from inside. It sounded like men's voices. Maybe they would tell her what was going on. Maybe she'd even see someone she knew, and realize what a wild, amazing trick had been pulled on her.

Suddenly, from behind, a voice shouted at her. She turned to see a huge man standing on a nearby pier. He wore a filthy white shirt and black vest and scarred boots. At his waist hung a long leather sheath. Beside the man was a teenage boy, his clothes soaked. The man raised his hand. Anne thought, *Oh, good, he's going to tell me what this trick is all about.*

But the man was frowning, and his face was twisted and ugly. He began to run toward her, shouting, "Come here, you stinking gypsy! I'll teach you to chase off our cargo and steal our merchandise!"

Anne gasped. This man didn't know her; he thought she was a thief! She turned and ran, the toes of her Nikes digging divots in the dirt.

"Come here, I tell you!" the man screamed.

Anne ran toward the trees. There, she could hide. Her heart hammered wildly. Where *was* she? She couldn't let this man catch her!

She looked over her shoulder. The man was closing the gap between them, his long legs flying across the ground as if he were a high school track star. His face was horrid in its fury. Anne couldn't imagine what he would do to her if he caught her.

She made it into the trees, then bent low to crawl through a thick patch of bushes. Her heart was pounding so loudly, she just knew he would hear it. She crawled several yards on her hands and knees and then held still when she heard the man enter the woods. He cursed and kicked at the leaves and rocks on the ground when he realized she'd gotten away. Anne curled into a ball, holding her breath and gritting her teeth.

"Where are you, gypsy?" the man called. He paused, waiting.

Anne swallowed. In her own ears, the action sounded very loud.

"I'll catch you," he cried. She could hear him kicking around in the brush now, looking for her. "I never lose a runaway. I'm Randolph Ritchie, and I never, ever lose a runaway."

The man came closer, stepping through the under-growth, and poking into the bushes with something shiny and sharp.

Chop, chop. The shiny thing went up and down out of the ground, like an oil drill seeking an underground well.

Chop, chop.

It came closer. Anne could see it cutting through the brush and weeds in smooth, deadly strokes.

It was a sword.

"Oh, my God," Anne whispered.

The man was trying to find her with a sword. *And if he catches me,* she thought, *he might use that sword to kill me!*

In a move so quick and graceful her gym teacher would have been impressed, Anne sprang up from her hiding spot and kicked one of the man's booted legs out from under him. His eyes widened, and as he went down, he bellowed like a stuck bull.

Anne sprinted from the brush and out of the woods. "That will only make it worse for you, girl!" the man shouted after her.

Anne dashed behind an empty wagon that stood be-fore a small, narrow building with a poorly hinged door. She darted inside the building and pulled the door closed behind her. Pressing her ear to the door, she listened for the man. She still could hear him yelling. He sounded angrier than before.

Julie, where are you? her mind cried. *This is crazy! Why am I here? Who is this man trying to catch me?*

She listened. The man stopped shouting, but she knew he was out there. Looking down, she saw there was a wooden latch for the door. Quietly, she slipped it into place. She peered behind her and wrinkled her nose when she realized she was in an outhouse.

"Julie, where are you?" she whispered. The only answer was the croaking of distant spring frogs, and the muffled singing of the men in the other building. And she was alone in this insanity.

Four

"Fine, then," Julie said to herself. She shoved her hands into the pockets of her jeans and frowned. If Anne wanted to play games, she'd give her a little room to do it. But it didn't take the edge off her worry, or the irritation she felt toward her friend for leaving her alone.

There were more exhibits Julie wanted to see before it was time to get on the bus and return to school. She strolled back down the hall of the second floor, past the Weedy Sea Dragon, past the electric eel, past a small cluster of kids from her school who spoke briefly to her and then went back to staring into the aquarium with the lionfish. At the end of the hall was a door to a darkened room. The sign read "Creatures of the Deepest Sea." Here, Julie knew, she would get to see some of nature's strangest monsters, the fish with razor teeth and glowing antennae. As she walked through the door into the near-black of the room, she wondered if she could set up a tank like this in her closet at home. All it would take would be a few hundred thousand dollars.

Oh, well, she thought. *Someday.*

As her eyes adjusted to the faint light filtering in from the hall, and the purple-blue lights from the prey-attracting lures on the heads of the monstrous fish, Julie realized she was alone in the room. It was kind of neat, as though she was by herself at the bottom of the ocean, watching these creatures swim and gape, their killer jaws hanging open.

It must be this quiet, she thought, *at the bottom of the sea. Quiet and dark.* Even as one razor-toothed fish lured another to its death inside the wide mouth, there were no screams. Only silence.

And suddenly, in the quiet and dark, a cold, bony hand closed around Julie's ankle, and she screamed.

Five

Anne put her hand to her chest and tried to slow the beating of her heart. And then she said, "No." She frowned and stamped her foot. This was crazy. This wasn't real. The man after her was not real; this outhouse wasn't real. It couldn't be. She must have slipped on a slick spot on the aquarium floor, fallen and hit her head. She was certainly unconscious or dreaming, and the only way to stop it was to take control of her own nightmare. The only way to stop it was to confront it and deny any of it was true.

Licking her lips and tossing back her head, Anne unlatched the outhouse door, stepped outside, and cried, "None of this is real. I demand that it stop, and I command myself to wake up! Now!"

She closed her eyes, knowing that when she opened them she would be back with her school friends, surrounded by the friendly occupants of the watery tanks at the National Aquarium.

She opened her eyes. Staring back at her were the red, wild eyes of the man with the sword and filthy shirt. He grinned, his lower lip cracking and oozing blood.

"You silly pig," he said, as he yanked a length of rope from his waistband and grabbed Anne's hands in order to tie them together.

Six

Jumping backward, Julie pulled free of the cold grasp. She stumbled to the door of the dark room and out into the light of the hallway. A few other students standing nearby stared at her. Brenda Mills, a seventh grader who was in the science club with Julie, hurried over to her.

"Was that you screaming?" she asked.

Julie nodded and struggled to catch her breath. Then she said, "There's someone in there. He grabbed my ankle and scared me to death."

Brenda's face wrinkled in fear. "We should tell security," she said.

"Yes," agreed Julie.

"I'll go," said Brenda. "And you get away from this door and don't let anyone else go in there. It might be an escaped criminal or something."

Julie nodded, and stepped back across the hall to the balcony. Brenda ran off while the other students who had been with her just stared.

Where is Anne? Julie thought, now furious at her friend for leaving her alone.

Where could she . . . ?

Oh, no. Julie thought.

Anne's prank. Anne was going to hide and scare Julie when she least expected it.

Anne.

"It's Anne!" Julie said. The kids at the lionfish tank laughed at her outburst, shrugged, then turned back to the display. *Oh, great,* Julie thought. *Won't Anne be happy when a security guard yells at her for causing trouble.*

Julie walked across the hall to the door of the deep-sea creature exhibit room.

"Anne," she called softly. "I'm going to kill you for scaring me like that!"

There was no answer from inside the dark room.

"I swear, Anne, the security guard isn't going to be happy with you. We might even get kicked out of the aquarium. That'll make our parents *real* happy; they won't be able to wait to send us on other field trips."

No answer. The dark room was silent.

Julie's heart skipped a beat. If it was truly Anne in there, she would have answered by now. Julie hesitated, then whispered, "Anne?"

A soft groan came from the corner of the room. Julie thought, *It's someone hurt, or someone insane.*

Just then, a security guard tapped Julie on the shoulder. She jumped and gasped, then looked around at him. Brenda stood back, her eyes wide.

"Someone grab you in there?" the security guard asked.

Julie nodded. "I thought it was my friend playing a trick. Now I don't think so."

The security guard called out, "Whoever is in there, come out now."

No answer. The man patted his gun, which hung on his belt in a holster. "Come out now," he said more loudly, "or we'll have to take you out by force."

Again, there was no answer. The guard opened a panel on the wall by the door and flipped a master switch. Bright lights came on inside the deep-sea room. "I'm coming in," he said. Brenda came up beside Julie and grabbed her arm.

The guard stepped inside. There was silence, then he whistled long and low.

Julie pulled away from Brenda. She took a deep breath, and stepped into the room with the guard.

"Oh, my gosh," said Julie.

There, on the floor in a corner, was a girl of about twelve or thirteen. She was barefoot. Her dress was thin and torn. Tied around her head was a plain brown bandanna, and her dark brown skin was covered with sweat and chill bumps. She stared as if she were afraid someone might hit her.

"Who are you?" demanded the security guard.

The girl said nothing, but pulled back even farther into the corner. She held one hand to her chest, as if her hand was hurt. She looked from the guard to Julie, her dark eyes wide and unblinking.

Julie couldn't imagine why this girl was here, dressed like this, and hurt, too. The girl's fear showed so clearly on her face. Julie wanted to do something to help. She said to the security guard, "Let me talk to her. Maybe she's afraid of you."

The man frowned. "Afraid of me? Why?"

"You are in uniform. You're, well, older . . ." She hesitated, then said, ". . . than us. And, well, you're a man." She shrugged.

"If she doesn't have a ticket, we have to take her out," the guard replied.

"I know," said Julie. "But if you leave the room, I'll talk to her and find out who she is. Okay?"

"Well . . ."

"Okay, then," said Julie, to help the guard make up his mind. He nodded slowly, then walked out of the room. As Julie watched him go, she saw Brenda peeking through the door, her eyes as big as soup bowls.

"I'll be out in a minute, Brenda," said Julie.

"You don't need my help?" Brenda asked softly.

"No. Please go on."

Brenda's head disappeared from the door. Only Julie, the deep-sea fish in the tanks, and the girl in the corner were left in the room.

Julie stared at the girl. The girl stared at Julie. Then Julie said, "Hi. I'm Julie. Who are you?"

The girl said nothing, but her mouth twitched as if she wanted to speak.

Julie sat down in front of the girl, careful not to get close enough to scare her. "Are you here with a school group?" she asked.

The girl pulled her lower lip in between her teeth

and her eyebrows drew up. It looked as if she wanted to cry, but was doing everything she could not to.

"Are you here alone?" asked Julie. Maybe, she thought, this girl was slow, and didn't understand what she was being asked. In all her life, Julie had never seen such fear on someone's face. Julie tried again. "My name is Julie. What's your name?" She smiled, hoping to make it easier for the girl to trust her.

The girl looked at the floor, then at her hands against her chest. When she looked back up at Julie, she took a deep breath and whispered, "Millie."

It so surprised Julie when the girl spoke, that she nearly fell back. She braced herself with one hand beside her on the floor and said, "Are you with a group, Millie?"

"Group?"

"Are you with a school? Are you with your family? How did you get here?"

Millie said, "I ran." She looked at Julie, then at the door, then at the light above their heads. She squinted and then shook as if she were very cold.

"Ran? What do you mean?"

Millie loosened one hand from her chest, and lifted a finger to point uneasily at Julie. She said, "Are you a runaway?"

"What?"

"Or are you a free girl?"

"A free girl? What do you mean?" Julie asked. This was so weird. If only Anne would come back from playing her stupid prank she could help Julie figure out what was going on.

"Free," said Millie. Her eyes closed for a moment, and when she opened them, she seemed tired and resigned. "Is this the North? I ran to be free, and I ain't going back no more."

This girl was out of her mind. Julie stood up and put her hand out for the girl to take. "Get up," she said. "I think we should go see my teacher, Ms. Cook. She'll help us figure out what to do."

Millie shook her head. "That man here a minute ago is a catcher, I can tell. I can't leave here or he'll take me back."

"Don't be afraid of him," Julie said. "He just works here. He makes sure people don't mess up the displays. He's not going to send you anywhere."

The girl in the torn dress and bandanna said, "You *must* be free to talk like this. You're free, ain't you? You won't let nothing happen to me, will you?" Her face, turned up to Julie's in the light, was so full of cautious trust that Julie knew she would do everything she could to take away this girl's fears.

"No," said Julie as Millie took her hand and slowly stood up on her bare feet. "I promise I won't let anything bad happen to you. I promise. Trust me."

They walked outside, into the hallway. Brenda and some girls from Julie's school were gathered in a cluster, whispering, pointing, and staring. When they reached the head of the escalator, Millie's eyes widened in new terror and she stepped back, but Julie just tightened her grip on Millie's hand.

"Trust me," she said again. And Millie got on the escalator, shaking, but trusting Julie.

As they rode down to the first floor, Julie looked at Millie carefully in the bright light of the aquarium. Why was this girl dressed like this? Why was she dirty, and why did one wrist seem to hurt her so badly? Julie looked down at the girl's bare feet, and for the first time, noticed that beneath the crusted mud, one foot was bleeding. Why was she dressed like, well, like a slave?

And why did this girl talk as if she had just come from another century?

Seven

"You don't have any right to do this to me!" Anne shouted, jerking her hands down and out of the ugly man's grasp. But he was quick, and before she could turn to run, he drove his fist into her stomach and she doubled over, coughing and gasping with pain. There were stars in the corners of her vision.

"Rights?" he said, pulling her hands back together and binding them with the rope he'd taken from around his waist. "What's this talk about rights? I have a right to protect my merchandise. Knocking Charles in the water and then chasing off the cargo! I have a *right* to catch a thieving gypsy and do what I want with her." The rope was knotted and strung around to draw her hands up behind her.

Anne tried to stand straight. The man laughed and spit on the muddy ground. "You better know not to give Randolph Ritchie a hard time," he said. "Don't nobody fight with me and win, not no man and especially not no silly pig of a girl. I can make you do whatever I want. Watch!"

He suddenly jerked on the end of the rope and Anne stumbled forward. With her hands behind her, she could barely keep her balance, but she was able to get her feet beneath her so she didn't fall. She took a breath, and stared up at the man, looking him straight in the eye.

"I don't care who you are," she said, her voice slow and trembling, but determined. "I don't care who you think you are. You have to let me go. You can't do this to me."

"Watch me," said the man. He turned and strolled toward the wooden building where men were singing. Anne had no choice but to hurry after him, her stomach still cramping from the blow, her mind still reeling with the confusion and fear of this place. She wanted to believe she had eaten something at lunch that had caused a severe, hallucinatory reaction. But as the man jerked on the rope and her wrists were cut with the rough material, and as she stepped into a wet hole full of mud and horse manure, she knew she was really *here*.

She was really in danger.

She was really alone.

The man took Anne onto the sloped front porch of the building and walked to the door. Closer now, Anne could hear that some of the singing men were clearly drunk. Randolph Ritchie tugged the end of the rope and Anne stumbled toward the door. Who was in the building, singing and drunk? Were these men just like Randolph Ritchie? What were they going to do to her?

Randolph pushed open the door and pulled Anne inside.

The room was large and cold. At long tables were seated men of all ages, from teenagers to men with long, unbrushed gray hair and beards. They sang and shouted and burped, laughing at themselves and each other. They were dressed in dirty shirts and muddy boots; many wore floppy hats. The smell inside the room was thick and raw, heavy with whiskey, sweat, and filth. Anne's stomach tightened.

On the tables sat dented tin mugs and bottles of brown and clear liquids. There were plates of biscuits and slabs of meats and potatoes. The only utensils were knives, with which the men stabbed the meat and potatoes before sticking the food into their mouths.

Randolph Ritchie drew his sword and smacked the blade across the end of one table. Only a few men stopped eating and looked at him, so he smacked the table with the blade again. The laughing and talking quieted. The men turned and looked at Randolph.

"Was down to my boat a bit ago," he said, "letting my boy load new merchandise. And what happens? The cargo gets away, my boy Charles nearly drowns in the water, and this gypsy girl talks to me like she thinks she's got rights!"

The eyes of the men turned to Anne. Some of them sneered, and several laughed, deep and mean laughs. Some watched Randolph Ritchie as if they hated him, and wanted nothing at all to do with him.

One old man with white hair and a poorly trimmed beard, sitting at the end of the table next to Randolph, wiped crumbs from his chin and nodded slowly.

"Looks like a gypsy, I tell you the truth. Have you ever seen such clothes in your life? She think she's a boy?"

Several men laughed.

"Don't know," said Randolph. He pulled at the sleeve of Anne's sweater, and then tapped her lower leg with his boot. "Never seen such an outfit. What type of gypsy is you, girl?"

Anne looked at the sword and at the rows of men who glared and grinned at her. She said, "I'm not a gypsy. I'm an eighth grader at Braunbeck Middle School."

Randolph tipped his head back and howled. Anne shivered and tried to step back, but the rope was held tightly.

"What's a eighth grader?" Randolph said, bringing his face up close to Anne's. "What's that, gypsy pig? You talking double-speak with me? You trying to cast gypsy spells with your double-speak?"

"They'll do it," said the white-haired man. "Gypsies will talk rings around you, I know. A gypsy man stole my mare last year when his woman tried to tell me a fortune. The fortune didn't make sense, but when I went out the tavern to the hitching post, my horse was gone. Then it made sense. Caught the man not long after." The white-haired man took a bite of a hard roll. "And we hung 'em both for horse stealing."

Randolph said, "What you trying to steal off the dock, girl? We got lots of men that ship goods from this port. Wheat, tobacco, corn, all going to Europe. You stealing food, girl?"

Anne thought, *If they think I'm stealing, they'll hang me.* Her heart pounded against her ribs as if it wanted to pop out. She licked her lips and said slowly, "Just listen to me. My name is Anne Ferguson. I'm thirteen years old, and I go to Braunbeck Middle School on the west side of Baltimore. I don't know how I got here, but I'm not a gypsy. I'm not a thief. I've never stolen a thing in my life."

"You lie," said Randolph. "Girls don't go to school. Gypsies don't go to school, either! What do you take me for, a fool?"

Anne felt tears rim her eyes, but she gritted her teeth so that the teardrops wouldn't fall. She said, "I'm not lying. Just listen to me, please."

Randolph spun on his heel and dragged Anne to a chair against the wall. "Enough of this babble," he said. "Sit down!" He shoved Anne back and she dropped onto the seat with a gasp. Taking the end of the rope, he wrapped it about the back of the chair and tied it. "Not a word now," he said, jamming his finger in Anne's face. "I've things to do 'fore we set sail in the morning, and no time to deal with the likes of you."

Anne looked away from him, glancing down at the floor and the filth that lay there. If only some of the men would help her. If only those who seemed to hate Randolph Ritchie would stand up to him. *But,* she thought, *they probably think I'm a thief, too.*

On the floor, a small gray mouse skittered about, looking for crumbs. Anne wished she was small like the mouse and could run away through a crack in the wall.

Julie, this is real but it can't be, she thought. *If you think of me, will I come back? Please, think of me!*

The men returned to their laughing and drinking. Randolph sat at the end of a table, banging his fists for a young, nervous waitress who scurried from a small adjoining room with a tray full of new biscuits.

"You don't argue with him and you may get on all right," said a voice to Anne's left.

Anne looked around and saw the boy who had been standing on the pier with Randolph Ritchie. He stood leaning against the wall near her, his arms crossed, his gaze flicking back and forth between the men and Anne. He was about sixteen, with dark brown, uncombed hair and blue eyes. He was dressed as the other men were, with a dirty white shirt tucked into gray pants and a pair of old boots. Both his pants and shirt were soaking wet.

"What do you mean?" Anne asked him.

The boy held a finger to his lips as if to make her talk more quietly. Then, crossing his arms again, he said, "You don't want to make the catcher mad. Believe me, I've seen his wrath."

"Who are you?"

"Name's Charles Jennings."

"If you're careful and slow, Charles, you could untie me."

Charles frowned. "You think you could get away

from here without one of these fellows coming after you? You'd never even get through the door."

"It's worth a try."

"And losing your life is worth that try?"

Anne swallowed hard. "Why aren't you there, drinking with the others?" she asked.

"I don't like what the whiskey does to men," he said. He looked up at the ceiling, then back down at Anne. "Some it makes dull. Others, cruel. The last thing I want to be is a man like Randolph Ritchie."

"So why are you here?"

"I have to be."

"Why?"

Before Charles could answer, there was a roar in the crowd of men. Anne jumped in her seat and looked back to the tables. Randolph was standing up, holding a leather pouch over his head.

"You like that, then?" he called to the other men.

Several stood and raised their mugs and shouted, "Let's have it! Let's have the wager!"

The young waitress, a woman in her early twenties with a long skirt and apron and hair in a bun, held the empty tray to her chest and backed toward the door of the adjoining room. Her face was full of fear, but she said nothing.

"Come here!" shouted Randolph to the waitress. "You heard the wager, a gold coin for the winner, and I take my gambling seriously!"

"Please, no," said the waitress.

Randolph and the other men laughed. One shouted, "Leave the woman alone!" But Randolph ignored him.

"I'm Randolph Ritchie," said Randolph to the waitress. "And I never back down from a challenge, be it chasing a slave or wagering against a foolish man who doesn't know how skilled I am at so many things. I said come here, woman, and stand there against the front door."

The waitress shook her head. "No," she whispered.

Randolph drove his mug down on the top of the table, sending whiskey upward in a dark spray. He stood and strode over to the waitress. He held his palm up before her face. "Johnny McCray," he said. "This your pub, and this your workerwoman. I pay a good price to spend my time here at your place when I'm resting in Baltimore's harbor. You going to let this woman spoil our fun, or are you going to have her do what I've asked?"

A short man with thin gray hair stood from his place at a table and said, "Lorna, you do as Mr. Ritchie has asked or you'll be out in the streets. He won't hurt you. He's very clever and precise when throwing a knife."

Anne looked at Charles then back at the waitress. Had he said *knife?*

"Randolph makes bets all the time," whispered Charles. "He likes it almost as much as he likes his whiskey."

The waitress put the tray she was holding on a table and, with eyes batting back tears, followed Johnny McCray to the front door. She clenched her fists at her side and closed her eyes. Randolph walked over and stood ten feet in front of her. "Give me the blade," he said, holding out his hand but not taking his eyes off the waitress.

Johnny McCray took a small, sharp knife from one table and handed it to Randolph.

"Now," Randolph said, and all the men in the room stopped talking. It was so quiet, Anne could hear her blood beat. "The wager was a gold dollar to the man who can throw the knife the closest to this girl's ear without nicking it. Is it understood?"

There was mumbling among the men, and most of them nodded. Several, clearly upset by the wager, slammed down their mugs and walked out the back door.

"I'll give it first go," said Randolph. He squinted one eye, held up the knife, and then flung it toward the girl. Anne shut her eyes and waited for a scream. There was none. The men burst into chuckles, and Anne opened her eyes again. The knife was in the door, three inches from the side of the waitress's head. Her eyes were still closed. She held her apron in her fists, and it was twisted into a ball.

"Not bad for a start," said Randolph. He coughed and spit on the floor, then rubbed his bristly face. "Now, who goes next? There's a coin in it for you."

An old man with a bad eye stood up and took the knife from the door. Randolph pointed at the old man with a wink and a grin, but the old man said, "Back home in the wilderness west of here, I can still pick a mockingbird off a pine bough while riding my horse at full gallop."

"We'll see, old man," said Randolph.

The old man stood where Randolph had stood. He cocked his head to one side, staring hard at the waitress with his one good eye. Then, before Anne could turn her head, he flicked the knife and it whistled in the air. It thumped and pierced the wood in the same place where Randolph's try had landed.

A few other men tried their luck after that, but they all were farther than Randolph and the old man's three inches. Then Randolph said, "The old man and I will have to have a last go."

This is crazy! Anne thought.

The old man rubbed the blade in his fingers as if warming it for good luck. Then he tilted his head again and threw the knife. The waitress gasped as it cut through the edge of her skirt and pinned the cloth to the door.

"You cut?" the old man asked.

The waitress shook her head, silent tears flowing down her cheeks.

"But it ain't her ear," said Randolph. "I wouldn't want to be hunting with you, old man. You'd just as likely throw the knife at me, thinking I was a buck!"

The old man snorted, and Randolph went to the door and pulled the knife free. Then he backed up, aimed the knife and said, "All you who tried get your coins in hand. They'll be mine in a matter of seconds."

And with that, he let the knife fly. The waitress

screamed. The knife bit the wood so close to her face that Anne thought she would see blood.

But there was none.

Randolph and the old man went to the door and studied the knife, while the waitress whimpered and shook.

"Ah, see there?" said Randolph. "A hairbreadth! Couldn't get a thread through the space, and she's not in the least harmed!"

The men let out a cheer, and those who had wagered against Randolph gave him their coins.

Randolph took a long swig from his mug, then slammed it onto the table. He wiped his mouth with his sleeve, then turned to Anne and Charles.

"Think it's time we took this gypsy below deck with the other cargo," he said.

Charles pushed away from the wall, and, without looking at Anne, he said softly, "Yes, sir."

Randolph drew his sword from his sheath and cut the rope away from the back of the chair where Anne sat. Then he jerked her upward and, with Charles following, dragged her back outside, where the afternoon crickets chirped and the distant horses whinnied and the water of the bay sloshed back and forth against the muddy bank.

Eight

Ms. Cook, a pretty teacher in her thirties with short blond hair, sat in a chair next to Julie and Millie, one hand out as though she were pleading with Millie to talk.

"Millie," she said, "it really would be easier on everyone if you would just tell us what happened to you. We don't want to hurt you; we want to *help*. We have to know where you came from so we can get you back safe and sound."

These words only made Millie pull farther back in her chair and draw her bare feet up into the seat.

Julie, Millie, and Ms. Cook were in a small meeting room next to the aquarium's gift shop. A security guard had said it would be a good place to try to talk to the girl.

But since they'd left the second floor, Millie had said nothing.

Ms. Cook said, "Julie, what did she say to you upstairs?"

"Well . . ." said Julie. She knew that what Millie had said sounded crazy, and for some reason, she didn't want Ms. Cook to think Millie was out of her mind, so she only said, "She said that she was running away."

"Ah," said Ms. Cook. "I see." She leaned close to Millie and tried to take her hand. Millie pulled her hands away and held them around her waist. Again, Julie noticed that one seemed to hurt her very badly.

"Millie," Ms. Cook said, "please talk with us. If you don't, we'll have no other choice but to call protective services."

Millie looked quickly at Julie as if to ask, what is that?

Julie shrugged. "Ms. Cook is right," she said. "Millie, we don't know what else to do. Trust me."

Millie licked her lips.

"Trust me," said Julie.

Millie loosened one hand long enough to wipe at her eyes, then she whispered, "I want to get to New York. To my cousins; they already got there. They's free, you know? I ran away from the Lawton Plantation in South Carolina. But I got stopped at the Maryland border. If I got over that border, I'd be a free girl. Maryland's south, Pennsylvania's north. Pennsylvania's free." The girl hesitated. Then she said, "But I got caught. Caught and brought to Baltimore to be taken back to the plantation."

Ms. Cook looked at Julie. Her expression showed that she, too, thought Millie had lost her mind.

Millie went on. "Randolph Ritchie was getting ready to put me on his boat to take me back to South Carolina, but then . . ." Millie looked at the floor and took a long breath. "But then I tripped and woke up and I was here. But I don't know where here is."

"I see," said Ms. Cook. She stood up from her chair and patted Julie on the arm. It was clear she didn't see any more than Julie did. "Julie, I think protective services will have to take it from here."

Julie nodded.

"I'll go make the call," Ms. Cook said. "Will you be all right here? Do you want to sit with Millie? Should I send in someone to stay with her so you can visit the rest of the aquarium?"

Julie looked at Millie, then said, "No, I'll stay with her. I promised her she could trust me."

"You'll be all right?"

"Yes," said Julie. "I'm sure I will be."

Ms. Cook went out of the small room. Julie looked at Millie, and Millie looked at Julie.

"What's wrong with your hand?" asked Julie.

Millie said softly, "Wrist is broke."

"It is? We should call a doctor, you know," said Julie. "That has to hurt something awful. How did you break it?"

"Fell when the dogs was after me," said Millie.

I should have known she'd say that, Julie thought.

"Who is protective services?" asked Millie.

"Oh," said Julie, "really nice people who will talk with you and take you home, I think."

Millie suddenly sat straight up in her chair. Her feet hit the floor. "Home?" she said. "Send me home? You told me a lie! Please don't have anyone send me home!"

"Oh, no," Julie pleaded, "just listen to me for a minute!"

But she didn't have the chance to finish what she was going to say, because Millie ran out of the room in a flash. Julie was left standing with her mouth open and her hand stretched out.

A moment later, Ms. Cook came back into the meeting room. "I forgot my purse," she said. "I know, I'd forget my head . . ." She picked up the blue bag she'd left on the floor beside a chair. "Now I'll go call . . ." She stopped and looked at Julie.

"Where's Millie?"

Julie stared out the door. "She left."

"She did? Where did she go?"

"I'm not sure," Julie said. Millie had begged Julie not to have her sent home. Maybe it would be better for Ms. Cook not to make the call after all. Maybe Millie was running away from an abusive family and that's why she was the way she was. Social services would probably only take her back there. "I think she remembered where she was supposed to be."

Ms. Cook looked concerned. "She seemed very confused to me."

"Well," said Julie, "I think she saw someone she knew out in the hall. She'll be all right. We don't have to call."

"Hmm. Well, then, I guess I have one less thing to worry about, don't I?"

"I guess," said Julie.

Ms. Cook sighed and walked out of the office. Julie sighed, too, and followed.

Nine

The dock creaked with the weight of the three of them, Anne, Charles, and Randolph Ritchie, as Randolph took them to the gangplank that crossed the water and led up to the deck of a wooden sailing ship.

Randolph, wildly drunk, sang loudly and off-key as they moved out across the dark water on the edge of the harbor.

> "Out Patapsco River,
> 'Round Fort McHenry's wall,
> Take them to the ocean,
> Back go one and all!"

Charles hung back, walking behind Anne with hands in his pockets and his head down. Anne stared in terror at the ship they were getting ready to board. Randolph had said he was going to put her below deck with the other cargo. What was the other cargo?

What was he planning to do to her?

"You just keep shuffling along back there," Randolph called over his shoulder, "and I'll jerk you so hard you'll go in the bay. Won't bother me none to see you sinking like a stone with your hands behind your back."

Anne walked a little faster.

They made their way up the gangplank, a narrow piece of wobbly board with thin, wooden footholds every two feet. It was hard to see where she was stepping; Anne tried to stay in the center so she didn't accidentally step off the edge. She stumbled once, and Charles caught her from behind. When she was steady, he put his hands back into his pockets. Finally, they stepped off the end of the gangplank and down onto the deck of the sailing ship.

"Well," said Randolph as Charles jumped down to the wooden flooring, "let's have us a lantern, or do you think you'll be able to see in the dark like bats?"

Charles hurried over to a large beam that rose from the deck and picked a lantern off a nail. He fumbled with the glass globe, struck a strange, long match against the beam, and lit the wick. In a moment, the lantern glowed yellow. Charles brought it over and stood beside Randolph.

Randolph grinned at Anne and made a sweeping motion from right to left. "This is my sweet *Sallie M.,*" he said. "My beautiful little runaway ship. I've been catching runaways for years now. They all try to get north, you know. Try to cross the Maryland border to Pennsylvania. Once they get out of Maryland they're free. But I'm good at my profession. I am quick and my dogs are quick. Many a slave owner in the South has not only paid me the reward offered for the return of the slave, but has invited me to dinner for my trouble!"

Anne felt the ship beneath her feet shift with the movement of the water, and she felt as though she might throw up.

Randolph went on talking. "I'm the best catcher of 'em all. Chase them down, bring them here to Baltimore's harbor, ship them home to their owners. I don't slip in my job. I don't fail in my aim. Am I right in what I say, Charles?"

Charles, standing near Anne with the lantern over one arm said, "Yes."

"Take a good look," said Randolph. "Then it's down with the other cargo for you until we sail south in the morning."

Anne looked around. The ship's deck was about twenty feet long and fifteen feet wide. Several beams rose up from the deck, bearing furled sails. On one end of the deck was a boxy shack with a door. On the other end was a raised deck and a steering wheel. In the center of the deck was a trapdoor. Down there, she knew, was the other cargo Randolph had talked about. It was down there he wanted to put her.

"Enough of this, now," said Randolph. "I think our little gypsy understands what is going on. Charles, take her down and secure her with the others. I've got some ciphering to do before the sun goes down."

Charles nodded. He took the end of the rope from Randolph and led Anne to the trapdoor. He kicked the door back. It flipped over and slammed to its side.

"And . . ." said Randolph. Both Charles and Anne turned to look at him. "If there is another escape, it'll be more than a finger this time." Randolph chuckled, then opened the door to the shack and went inside.

Anne glanced at Charles, who immediately shoved his left hand into his pocket.

Then he said, "Get down there."

Anne looked at the black square hole that led to the lower deck, and at the rickety ladder that disappeared down into that hole.

"I can't go down there," she said.

Charles sighed heavily. "You ain't got a choice. Neither do I. Move."

Charles stepped over the edge of the hole and caught the ladder. He jerked on the rope, and Anne followed, Charles's hands on her legs and back as she awkwardly descended without the use of her own hands.

Finally, the two reached the stinking, lightless unknown.

Ten

Julie stood in the crowd outside the National Aquarium, watching the people strolling along the walkways on the banks of the Patapsco River, and moving in and out of the shops of Harborplace. Many of the people were tourists, carrying bright plastic shopping bags full of souvenirs. Some seemed to be natives of Baltimore, standing around in their suits and nice work clothes, chatting casually. Other people jogged through the brisk air, wearing shorts and tee shirts and headphones. The Inner Harbor was a busy, modern place with busy, modern people doing busy, modern things.

Would a confused young girl, dressed like someone from a hundred years ago, *survive* in such a place?

It was nearing five o'clock, and the day had turned cold, with heavy gray clouds hanging in the sky. Julie walked down to a dock that led to a double-decker tourist boat and looked around. She knew it had been a bad idea to go outside the aquarium. Ms. Cook hadn't seen her sneak out to find Millie. *At least I have a ticket stub,* she thought. *They'll have to let me back inside.*

But first, she had to find Millie.

She had told Millie to trust her, and something deep inside her couldn't just let the strange girl disappear before she did all she could to help her. The girl was troubled and hurt, and Julie knew that she was the only one who could *really* help her now.

"Millie!" she shouted, but she knew the girl would not answer her even if she heard her. She was too afraid for that. Julie would have to find her and take her back to the aquarium. Then, at five-thirty, when Anne finally decided to show up and stop her stupid games, the two of them could decide together how they could best help Millie.

The gangplank to the tourist boat shuddered and creaked, then was lowered slowly until it came in contact with the pier. A bouncy guide dressed in sailor whites trotted across the plank and stepped onto the pier, then moved aside to let a stream of tourists get off the boat. Julie watched the people as they walked past her. Mothers and fathers helped little children step onto the pier; young couples walked arm in arm, looking more at each other than where they were going. Three elementary school-aged boys got off the gangplank and sat down on the side of the pier to drop popcorn crumbs from a striped bag into the water and call for fish to come eat them.

"Millie," Julie said quietly. "Where have you gone?"

The guide in the sailor suit waved at Julie. "Hey, this was our last tour for the afternoon," she said. "We don't go out again until nine o'clock, when we have our moonlight tour of the harbor."

"That's okay," said Julie. "I don't want a tour."

The guide shrugged and spun around. She walked back across the gangplank onto the boat and went inside the cabin.

Julie folded her arms across her chest. *Forget it,* she thought. This was all too weird to try to sort out. She'd go back into the aquarium and find Anne and just forget this whole, strange thing. If Millie didn't want to be found, then she didn't want to be found. It didn't look like there was much Julie could do about it.

The tour guide came back out of the cabin with another guide, a teenage boy, wearing a similar outfit. They were followed by an older man, probably the captain, who wore a tired-looking blue hat with gold braid. The three stepped onto the pier, and the girl strung a chain across the front of the gangplank. A sign hung from the chain: "Closed Until Our Moonlight Trip. Open 9:30 P.M." The man and the two young guides then hurried past Julie to the shore. Julie shoved her hands into the pockets of her jeans and walked slowly after them.

As she stepped off the pier, she suddenly turned back to look at the tourist boat. Could Millie have hidden there?

No way, Julie told herself. The boat was carefully watched by the guides. No entrance without a ticket. No . . .

And Julie gasped.

Something was happening to the boat. It seemed to shimmer, like ripples on a pond. Julie rubbed her eyes and looked again. It was evening, and the sun was beginning to set. Surely she was just seeing things. But the rippling continued, making Julie feel dizzy.

And then, it was there.

Lying over the surface of the tourist boat like some giant classroom transparency, was the image of another boat. A sailing ship, actually. A rough ship with sails tied to tall beams and a narrow gangplank leading from the pier to the deck of the boat.

"What is this?" Julie whispered.

What it seemed to be was a ghost ship, docked off the pier at the harbor, waiting for its crew and cargo to come aboard so that it could sail off into the Atlantic Ocean. Julie looked around her, wanting to see if anyone else nearby was seeing what she was seeing. But no one else seemed to notice. Even the people who were looking straight at the harbor and the tourist boat were acting normal.

Julie looked back at the boat. Now, she could see ghostly images of people climbing the gangplank to the sailing ship. There was a man, dressed in a white shirt and boots, a sword hanging from his belt. There was a boy in the rear, his arms crossed, his head hanging down. And between the two, her hands tied behind her back, was a girl.

A girl dressed in a sweater and jeans. A girl with long red hair.

Julie took a step forward, her eyes widening, her mouth open as if she wanted to scream but couldn't.

The girl going up the gangplank to the old sailing ship was Anne!

"Impossible," Julie whispered. Heart pounding, she took another step forward and squinted, trying to make the ghostly vision disappear.

But the shimmering image remained. Julie stared in horror as a man, a boy, and her best friend, tied up and stumbling, stepped over the rail of the specter-ship and down onto the deck.

Julie put her hand to her mouth and closed her eyes. *Anne,* she thought, *what's happened? Where are you? When are you?*

When she opened her eyes, the ghostly image was gone. Only the double-decker tourist boat sat in place on the water, waves lapping its sides.

Waves that seemed to know what was going on but wouldn't tell. Waves that seemed to be laughing.

Eleven

The lower deck of the ship was hot and steaming, and rank with a terrible mixture of smells—rotted food, dead rats, human wastes, and, worst of all, fear.

Charles had gone down the ladder before Anne, keeping the lantern, still turned low, hooked over one elbow and one hand against her back so she wouldn't lose her balance. Anne stepped off the bottom rung of the ladder onto the floor. She did not move. She was afraid to step forward, fearful of what she might see or touch.

There were sounds down in the hold. Dreadful sounds that she had only heard in her nightmares. There was a scratching sound—live rats and mice, she thought. There was the sound of the waves smacking the sides of the ship, and the painful creaking of the wood. And there were human sounds of soft crying and harsh coughing. There was the sound, it seemed, of death.

"Let me turn this up," said Charles, his face in darkness.

There was a sputtering of light, and the lantern shone more brightly. The lower deck was now washed in faint light. Finally, Anne could see some of the other cargo Randolph had mentioned.

People were the cargo.

There were people sitting along the slanted walls; many leaned forward, staring at their feet. Others sat against the beams that rose from the floor to the ceiling. Others were lying out on the bare floor. Men, women, teenagers, and children—all black, all tied to each other and to heavy metal rings in the walls and floors. None looked up at her. Some were silent. Others seemed to be whispering to themselves. Some of the children cried weakly.

"What's going on?" Anne asked, stunned, her voice low and broken.

"Cargo," said Charles. He put the lantern onto a nail on the center beam. "Taking them back south in the morning."

Anne felt the floor buckle beneath her, and it wasn't because of the waves. Her head spun.

"You have to come over here and let me tie you to this." Charles tapped a steel ring on the wall, two feet from the floor. He wanted to tie Anne up like all these other people.

"No," said Anne.

"You have to," Charles replied. "I can't do nothing about it. Randolph's got the sword. I ain't got nothing."

Anne shook her head. "No," she repeated. "I won't. You can't do this to me."

A girl of about ten, seated on the floor, her hands tied to her ankles, turned and looked up at Anne. Her face was streaked with tears and dirt, but her eyes were set and sure.

"Good for you, sister," she said quietly. "Be brave and stay strong."

Anne said, "Who are you?"

The girl said, "My name don't matter now. After a while a lot of things don't matter. But freedom does. Freedom matters more than a name."

"Freedom," whispered several voices from people around the floor and against the walls.

"Be quiet," said Charles. "If Randolph hears this, you know what will happen."

The bound woman beside Anne said, "What can he do he ain't already done? Beat us to death? Freedom matters more than life. Many slaves have rebelled. That was their way. We ran away. That was ours."

"Freedom," whispered the voices.

Anne said, "Charles, you know Randolph is drunk. He might be asleep by now. We could all get away. You have the power to set these people free!"

"Don't talk like that!" In the lantern light, Charles's face drew up in fear. "Randolph don't sleep yet. It's not even sundown. He'll be going over his captain's journal in his cabin, thinking about tomorrow."

"Freedom," whispered the voices.

"Charles, *please.*" Anne stepped away from the ladder and toward the boy. She could feel the eyes of those who were chained upon her.

"Randolph has the best dogs," Charles argued. "You don't know him. You don't know what he can do!"

"Charles, *please* do what's right."

"I can't."

Anne looked at the faces of the people on the floor. Most she couldn't see well because of the bad light, but she knew they were watching her, waiting, hoping. Part of her felt as though she was in a movie, and that someone had forgotten to give her a script. But part of her knew this was not make-believe.

"Charles, let us go," she said quietly.

Charles suddenly rushed toward Anne. His mouth was twisted with anger. His eyes were pinched with torment. "I can't!" he shouted. He pulled his left hand from his pocket and held it up before Anne's face. The pinky on the hand was gone, with only a raw, bloody stub in its place. "I lost this finger to Randolph's sword today when a runaway slave got away from me. He'd caught her by the river, and brought her to Baltimore with the others. While he was on the shore, fixing a broken lace on his boot, and I was getting ready to load the girl on the boat, I got knocked overboard and she disappeared. I was talking with her, and suddenly, into the water I went. And she just vanished, like she'd never been there at all. *You* know that. *You* is the one who tried to save her. Randolph didn't believe me; he thought I let the girl go, and he cut my finger off for losing her. Ran up to me, pulled out my hand, and sliced the finger off right there on the pier! Next time, I'm not sure *what* he'll do to me."

Anne turned her face away from Charles's bloody hand. "I didn't knock you in the water," she answered softly. "I never saw the girl you're talking about. And I've never been here before."

"You got to do what I say or there'll be more pain to pay," Charles said. "Bad pain. Randolph don't care about crying or screaming. To him, it's like music."

Charles grabbed the end of the rope and pulled Anne to the steel ring on the wall. He tied her to the ring. Anne slid down beside a small woman. She wore a long, torn dress. She was barefoot and silent.

"I'm sorry I couldn't help," Anne said.

The woman slowly turned her head to face Anne. The understanding in her face was beautiful. "It's all right, child," she said. "Slavery and servitude ain't long for this country. I seen it in a dream."

"Please," said Anne, "what year is it?"

"Why, it's already 1849," said the woman. "America is a good country. This badness won't last forever."

Anne nodded, a tear falling from her eyes to the filthy floor. "You're right," she said. "You really are right."

The woman smiled at Anne, then turned her face down and shut her eyes.

But that doesn't help us now, Anne thought. She put her head on her knees. "We have to get free," she whispered. "We have to get free from this place."

Twelve

"Ms. Cook," said Julie, "have you seen Anne?"

Ms. Cook stood beside the seal pool, her hand in the air, counting students. "What?"

Julie let out a breath of air in frustration. If Ms. Cook *had* seen Anne, then the vision Julie had seen outside at the pier had been just a wild trick of her mind. "Have you seen Anne?" she repeated.

"That's forty-six," Ms. Cook said. "Oh, I wish the parent chaperones would hurry back here so we can get a final count. It's five thirty-five, and we should all have been here by now, ready to go."

All around the outdoor seal pool, students from Braunbeck Middle School were gathered. Brenda and some other girls were giggling and whispering to each other. Jerry, looking as cute as ever, Julie thought, stood leaning against the side of the pool, while John and Tim did ridiculous seal impressions, impressing no one but themselves. If this had turned out to be a normal field trip on a normal day, Julie would have made herself walk over to the seal pool and hope she could think of something good to say to Jerry when she got there.

But it wasn't a normal day. It was the strangest day Julie had ever experienced.

"Ms. Cook, please," said Julie.

Ms. Cook turned to Julie. Her mouth was set in a tight line, and she didn't look happy. Well, Julie couldn't worry about that now. *"What,* Julie? I've got to get everybody together. What do you need?"

"I need to know if you've seen Anne."

"Anne Ferguson? No, not recently. She'll show up," said Ms. Cook. "At least, she's one student who's usually responsible for being where she needs to be. I can count on her."

I'm not so sure, Julie thought. Aloud she said, "You don't understand, Ms. Cook. I really need to know if anyone has seen her in the past half hour or so."

"I haven't," said Ms. Cook. "But she's probably buying a souvenir. Just don't *you* go away from here, now. I'm trying to keep count."

Ms. Cook then walked over to a set of glass doors that led back into the aquarium, put her hand to the glass, and looked in, trying to spy other students who had yet to make it to the seal pool.

Julie trotted over to Brenda and her friends. "Have you seen Anne?"

"You're still looking for her?" Brenda asked between bites of a candy bar. "Man, that's pretty rude of her to just run off like that."

"So, you haven't seen her?"

"No. But we didn't exactly go through the whole place. We ended up hanging out at the gift shop, watch-

ing the really cute guy who was selling the postcards,"
Brenda explained. She looked at the other girls in her
group. "You guys didn't see Anne Ferguson, did you?"

The girls all shook their heads. Julie felt her heart sink
and her skin prickle. She then took a breath and strode
toward Jerry, Tim, and John. They had toured the entire
aquarium, she was sure. Even though talking with Jerry
still made her nervous, the thought that what she'd seen
at the waterside made her *more* than nervous.

"Jerry," she said, and Jerry turned from watching
his two friends make goofy noises.

"Yep?" he asked.

"Remember I was looking for Anne a little while ago?
I was wondering if you saw her anytime after that?"

"You mean since you asked me up on the second
floor?"

"Yeah. She's really disappeared. I think something's
happened to her."

Jerry's eyebrows went up. "You mean, like she's
been kidnapped? Have you told Ms. Cook?"

"No, not exactly like kidnapped," Julie said. How
was she supposed to explain what she'd seen? Was she
losing her mind? "Like gone. Like vanished. Like not
here anymore, and I can't really explain what I mean
other than that."

Tim leaned over and said, "Hey, Julie, John and I
have a bet that your legs are so long, you can jump
from one side of the seal pool to the other. There's ten
bucks in it for you if you try!"

Julie made a disgusted face and looked back at Jerry. "You really haven't seen her, then, have you?"

"No," said Jerry.

"Come on, Julie." Tim hopped up on the side of the pool and circled his hand in her direction. "Come on up here. We want to see you jump over the seals. You *are* the tallest girl in eighth grade." He laughed and John nodded in agreement. He blew a huge bubble of gum and it popped all over his face.

"If you miss," John said, pulling gum off his face, "no big deal. The seals can toss you back on the side. They toss stuff around all the time. Rings, beach balls. Come on, Julie. Ten-dollar bet, what do you say?"

"Shut up, Tim," said Jerry suddenly. Then he said to Julie, "Have you told Ms. Cook? They can make an announcement over the intercom system."

"I told her that I hadn't seen Anne in a long time. She doesn't think anything's wrong."

"Maybe she's right," Jerry suggested.

Julie felt fear and frustration climb her spine like a pair of cockroaches. She gritted her teeth so she wouldn't yell. "She's *not* right," she said finally. "And I don't have time to try and prove it."

"Hey, Julie!" It was Tim. "Come on up with me! The seals are ready. Presenting Julie Sawyers, ladies and gentlemen, Seal Stunt Woman with Long Legs!"

"Shut up, Tim!" Julie cried. In a flash of anger, she planted the palms of her hands against the lower part of Tim's legs and shoved. Tim's arms flew out, his mouth flew open, and he tumbled off the side of the pool and into the water. There was a huge splash.

Braunbeck Middle School students raced in the direction of the splash, many of them screaming with laughter. Ms. Cook, still peering through the glass doors, turned, dropped her hand, and ran to the seal pool. Jerry stared at Julie with a mixture of surprise and admiration.

"What happened?" Ms. Cook shouted.

"Tim jumped in with the seals!" someone cried.

Julie backed away. She couldn't believe what she'd done, but she couldn't worry about it now. Nobody had seen Anne; nobody knew where she was.

Except Julie. She knew where Anne was. On a ghostly ship in the harbor, captive of two men in old-fashioned clothes. Much like the type of clothes she'd seen on Millie.

Like Millie.

Like the ragged, dirty clothes Millie had been wearing.

Yes! thought Julie. *Millie must have something to do with this. Millie might be the answer to this terrible puzzle!*

Julie glanced at the crowd by the seal pool, at the uniformed security guards swarming around, pushing kids back, trying to get to the side to help Tim out of the water. Brenda and her friends stood clutching each other, giggling so hard their shoulders shook. "Tim's such a moron!" Brenda laughed. "He couldn't stand up straight if someone gave him directions!"

If I find Millie, Julie thought, *I might be able to find Anne. I don't have any other choice.*

Julie looked over her shoulder toward the dark water of Baltimore's harbor and the boats that floated in the fading sunlight. *Anne,* she thought, wishing her friend could hear her thoughts. *I'm going to help you, no matter what it takes.*

And suddenly, a hand came down on her shoulder and spun her around. The face of a furious guard was pressed into hers. Julie's mouth fell open.

"I hear you're the one who pushed that boy into the pool," the man said. "You're in big trouble, young lady."

"But I . . ." Julie tried to step away but the guard's grasp on her shoulder was tight.

"There is no excuse for what you did," he continued. "I'm taking you to your teacher. We'll call your parents, and have this straightened out. This kind of behavior can't be ignored. It's dangerous to our animals."

"I didn't mean to do it! Let go of me!" Julie cried.

But the guard wasn't listening. He waved to another guard, who tapped Ms. Cook on the shoulder and pointed toward them. The look on Ms. Cook's face was painful to see.

Julie put her hands to her face. Now, she was going to have to explain the whole story to the aquarium officials and to her teacher.

Somehow, she didn't think they'd believe any of it. And Anne was still out there, stranded in some kind of time warp, in a danger Julie could barely imagine.

Thirteen

Anne's whole body ached. She had been tied to the steel ring in the wall of the ship for what seemed like a long time, and she was too frightened and in too much pain to sleep.

All around her, the captured runaways shuffled about anxiously, drifting in and out of sleep. No one spoke. They must have known, as Charles had said, that Randolph Ritchie could hear a termite at a mile's distance.

Charles was still below deck. He sat at the base of the ladder, his knees up, his chin resting on them. He stared out into space, barely seeming to blink. The lantern had been turned very low, and he was the only person clearly visible in the dim light. Charles's dark hair was tousled; a strand hung across his forehead, and the sides caught in the collar of his shirt.

"Charles," Anne whispered.

The boy's blue eyes turned toward her. His head hardly moved. "What?" he asked softly.

"What do you think about all this?"

"What do you mean, this?"

"Slavery. People owning people."

Charles scratched his neck, then sighed. He said, "I

hate it. It's so wrong. And it's not just because I'm bound to Randolph Ritchie. Even if I wasn't, I'd say it was wrong."

Anne tossed her head, throwing back a loose piece of hair. "What do you mean you're bound?"

"Three years ago, my daddy was in trouble," Charles explained. "A fire had burned our home down and damaged the public stable next to it. Even though our house was just a shack, all we had was gone. And two horses in the stable died. My mother went to work as a seamstress to help repay the cost of the horses. But that, along with my father's pay from the railroad, wasn't enough to pay for the horses as well as find a new home and new clothes. One night, my father was in a tavern, drinking to ease the worry. He met Randolph Ritchie."

Anne took a long, deep breath as she listened.

"Ritchie is a gambling man, I think you know now. My father got to talking with him. The two made a wager. I don't think my father even remembers exactly what the bet was; he was not in his right mind. If my father won the wager, he would receive twenty gold coins. This would be enough to pay for the horses, and maybe there'd even be a little left over for some dishes."

"What if Randolph won?"

Charles blew an angry, tired breath of air through his tight lips. "What do you think? Haven't you figured it out by now? If my father lost, he would give Randolph a boy to work for him for the next six years."

"You mean . . . ?"

"Yes," said Charles. "My father bet me. And he lost. I'm bound to Randolph until I'm nineteen."

"But," Anne argued, "that's not legal, is it?"

Charles shrugged. "Legal? I don't know if it is or not. But would that matter? My family is poor. People do what they must."

"But you stay with him."

"I have to. His dogs could catch me as quickly as they catch a slave. He feeds me. I have a bed. When I'm asleep, I dream of when I'm nineteen and free. Slavery is wrong, whether it involves a black man or a white."

"Most people don't think as you do?"

Charles said, "That's a silly question. We're in the South. Where are you from? New York? Pennsylvania? Are you from an abolitionist family?"

"No."

"Are you Quaker?"

"No, I'm a Catholic from Baltimore," Anne said. "My family moved here from Wisconsin two years ago."

"Wisconsin? Where is that?"

Anne ignored his question. "Charles, I don't know what has happened to me. The woman next to me here told me the year is 1849. Half of me refuses to believe it, but the other half tells me she's right. Somehow, I've come here, back in time from the 1990s. I don't know how I'm going to get back to where I came from."

One side of Charles's lip went up in a humorless

sneer. "Why do you say such a thing? I'm not dim-witted. I don't fool easily."

"I didn't say you did."

Charles put his face to his knees and was silent.

Anne took a breath. "Charles," she said, "did you say the slave girl just disappeared as you fell into the water? Disappeared like smoke into the air?"

Charles did not look up. "Yes," he said finally.

"And does that make sense to you?"

"No."

"Then if you can accept that, then accept what I'm telling you. I'm from the future, from a time when owning other human beings is against the law."

Charles raised his head. "It makes no sense."

"I know."

"Why did this happen?"

"I wish I knew," said Anne. "But I have to get home, back to where I belong. And I want all these people to go free." She paused, then said, "And I want you to go free, too."

"You expect too much."

"I can't expect less," Anne said fiercely. "If people expect less than what is right, what is right will never happen."

Suddenly, there was a crash on the upper deck. Anne cried out, as did several of the other tied people in the room. Then everyone looked up, waiting to see what had made the noise.

The trapdoor was thrown back, and a deep voice shouted from above.

"I got me a bet! Charles, have me a slave up here 'fore I can count to ten or I'll beat the soles of your feet 'til you bleed! You hear me?"

Anne looked at Charles. Charles stared up the ladder.

"You hear me, you worthless boy?" called Randolph Ritchie. "You want to be able to walk the rest of your life, you best have me a slave right now!"

"Charles, don't," Anne pleaded.

Charles hesitated. By the look in his eyes, Anne could see that he wanted to resist Ritchie's command.

But then Randolph said, "Not only your feet, boy, but the feet of all them that's tied below! And you know I keep my word!"

Then a soft voice from the corner said, "Charles, I'll go. Untie me and I'll be the one."

Anne looked to her left. An old man with short, curly white hair and a sunken face had spoken. He went on. "Take me up there. I'm old. Whatever he has planned, it don't matter to me. Take me and save these others."

"Oh, Toby," whispered the woman next to Anne.

"Charles!" shouted Randolph. "I'm counting! One, two, three . . ."

Charles stood and hurried to the old man. He untied the rope that attached the man to a foot clamp and then helped the man get up.

"Six, seven, eight," called Randolph. "Charles, have you forgotten I'm a man of my word?"

"I'm coming," Charles called back.

Charles glanced at Anne. "I don't have a choice," he said.

Anne looked down at the floor.

After a moment, she heard the ladder creaking, and Randolph said, "Ah, there, that's a good one. Up here, now, Charles, then you can go back with the others."

The old man grunted as he was taken up through the trapdoor. Then the trapdoor was slammed shut. Anne heard Charles's footsteps on the rungs as he descended.

"I didn't have a choice," Charles said. His voice was raspy with hopelessness.

The people in the darkness of the lower deck held their breath, listening for what was going to happen on the upper deck. Anne watched the ceiling, and watched those around her. She wanted to scream, to shake free of this nightmare. She wanted to break her ropes magically and take these people to her own Baltimore, where slavery was only an ugly word in the dictionary. But as she tugged on her ropes, they only cut into her arms, and they did not give way.

Then came the sound of a gunshot from above, and a loud, evil laugh. "Dance!" Randolph shouted. "I bet you could dance higher than that. You best prove me right!"

There was a hesitation, then another shot. More laughter, this time from Randolph and another man.

"Toby," said the woman next to Anne. "Please come back to us alive."

Another shot rang out. And Randolph shouted in glee. "James Anderson, I think you will owe me a gold piece after this wager is done!"

"This is wrong," Anne said.

"Load 'er up again, Ritchie," came the other man's voice from above. "He's spry for a codger!"

"This is wrong!" Anne screamed.

"Be quiet!" Charles shouted. He rushed to Anne and got on his knees in front of her. His breathing was heavy. "Be quiet or he'll do us all. Do you understand?"

"No." Anne didn't understand any of this. If only she could call for Julie to help her. Did Julie even know she was gone? Was Julie still roaming the aquarium, looking for new fish to add to her own tank?

Charles put his hand gently on Anne's arm. "You must understand," he pleaded. "Don't you?"

"Yes," said Anne finally.

Then the trapdoor opened with a bang. Charles stood and hurried back to the foot of the ladder to help Toby come down. In the dim light, Anne saw that the old man looked dazed.

"Toby," said the woman beside Anne, "you all right, honey?"

Toby could only cough. Charles led the man to the far side of the deck, into the shadows where Anne couldn't see him anymore.

From the trapdoor hole, Randolph called down, "Good choice, Charles! When old James saw that shriveled man he bet I could only make him dance a little. But I proved a good bullet is like a pretty woman; a set of feet will prance high with just a bit of encouragement. I got me another gold coin in the wager. Baltimore is a fine city, don't you think?"

Charles came out of the shadows and stood by Anne. He looked up at the trapdoor but said nothing.

"I said it's a fine city, don't you think?" Randolph's voice was sharp.

"It's a fine city," Charles replied. He shook his head and put his hands into his pockets.

"You and the rest of those animals down there be good and when I'm through getting this old crook to pay up for his wager, I may think about bringing down some supper for each of you."

Charles sighed.

"Ain't you going to say thank you?" called Randolph.

"Thank you," said Charles.

The trapdoor slammed shut.

"Charles," Anne said, "Baltimore *is* a fine city. It's always been a fine city. A few bad people don't destroy what's good. They just hurt it a bit."

Charles sat at the base of the ladder and put his head on his knees. "I don't want to hear it," he said.

Anne wished she had a watch. But if she did, would it work here in 1849?

There had to be a way to get out of here and back to her own time. She knew she was smart; she'd always gotten good grades in school. But, she wondered, did she have the kind of smarts it took to plan a life-and-death escape?

If ever there was a time to find out, it was now. She

didn't have much time to waste. If she wasn't free by
morning, she would be sailing south, to become someone's bound servant—or Randolph Ritchie's personal
maid.

Fourteen

It was almost six o'clock. Ms. Cook was furious. The departure of the Braunbeck Middle School kids had been delayed because of Tim's plunge into the seal pool. Parent chaperones had taken the other students to the buses to wait. But Julie was still in a security office with Ms. Cook, facing an angry assistant museum director.

"I know you are embarrassed by what has happened, Ms. Cook," said the assistant director, a tall, heavyset woman with glasses. "It's a shame a few students have to ruin an excursion for everyone."

Ms. Cook sighed loudly and crossed her arms. She continued to look at Julie as if she still couldn't believe what had happened. Julie couldn't believe it, herself. She had *never* done anything that had gotten her in big trouble like this. She was hurt that Ms. Cook was so angry. It wasn't as if Julie made a *habit* of pushing jerks off walls into seal pools!

The assistant director leaned against the small wooden desk in the center of the office and turned to Julie. "What do you have to say for yourself?" she asked. "Don't you have any respect for the animals we try so hard to care for here?"

"I love animals," Julie said. "I want to be a marine biologist when I grow up. All this was an accident."

"A lot of accidents aren't harmless," the assistant director replied. "Carelessness wouldn't make it any better if one of our seals had been hurt."

Julie crossed her arms and her foot began tapping nervously. What a waste of time this was. Anne was in danger, Julie needed to find Millie as soon as possible, and here she was, getting a lecture on respecting animals.

"Ms. Cook," Julie began, turning to her teacher, "what do you want me to do? Apologize? Then, I'm sorry. Say it'll never happen again? Believe me, it won't. Pay for any damage? I don't have much money but if there's a fine, tell me what it is and I'll take care of it. Can't we just get this over with?"

"The only way I can let this go is to talk with your parents while you are here with me," the assistant director said. "They need to know what happened. What is your phone number?"

"Wait," Julie cried. It was no use. She was going to have to tell them about Anne and the ghost ship. If they didn't believe her, then it really wouldn't make anything worse. But if they *did* believe her, maybe they would see that there was no time to lose.

"What?" asked Ms. Cook.

Julie took a deep breath. "It's about Anne. Listen to me, please. Remember, I'm not crazy. Anne's gone;

she's vanished. She was with me an hour and a half ago, and I haven't seen her since." Julie hesitated, then said, "I think she's gone to another time. When I last saw her she was like a ghost, all filmy and transparent. She was climbing onto a strange old ship with two men, dressed like they were from long ago. I don't have *time* to make any phone calls. I have to . . ."

"Julie!" cried Ms. Cook. "Don't you dare play games with us! I've never known you to lie. But then, I never thought you would do something like endanger animals. Drop this story at once!"

"I'm not lying!" Julie protested. "I *know* it sounds unbelievable, but you have to believe me, anyway."

"Julie, stop it this minute," Ms. Cook demanded. "Don't make things any worse than they already are."

Suddenly, there was the sound of someone clearing his throat. Julie's head spun around and there stood Jerry in the doorway. His hands were in his pockets, and his eyebrows were up in an expression of embarrassment.

"What do you want, Jerry?" asked Ms. Cook impatiently. "You are supposed to be on the bus with the others."

"Well . . ." Jerry stepped into the office. "I felt really bad, so I thought I better come straighten things out. Julie didn't push Tim into the seal pool. I did."

"What?" asked Ms. Cook.

"What?" asked the assistant director.

What? Julie thought.

"I was goofing around and dared Tim to get up on

the side. Maybe it looked like Julie pushed him in, but she didn't. I gave him a nudge and Julie was only reaching out to catch him so he wouldn't fall in. I can't let her take the blame for something I did."

"Well," said the assistant director.

"Don't make up a story, Jerry," Ms. Cook warned. "We already have one wild lie from Julie."

"It's not a lie, Ms. Cook," Jerry promised. "Julie was only asking if we'd seen Anne. Tim was being a major creep, as usual. I wouldn't blame Julie if she had pushed him in, but she didn't."

"Hmm." Ms. Cook looked at Julie, then Jerry. "I'm glad you decided to tell the truth, Jerry, but it sure took you awhile to decide to tell it."

"Sorry." Jerry winked at Julie.

I never knew he liked me, Julie thought. *He's taking the blame for something I really did. Maybe later, when all this is over, I'll be happy. But now, I can't even think about it. All I know is I owe him a really big favor!*

"You may go, then, Julie," said Ms. Cook. "And go back to the bus with the others. Tell them there's no need to wait for us. Parents are already at the school. Jerry can call his parents and they can pick him up from here. I'll stay with him."

Julie glanced at Jerry, and he raised his eyebrows a little.

"It's the least he deserves for this little prank," Ms. Cook went on. "Here, let me write a note for the chaperones." Ms. Cook took a piece of notebook paper from the desktop and quickly scribbled some lines.

Then she handed the note to Julie. "I understand that you're worried about Anne, Julie. I bet she's with the others by now. But if she isn't on the bus, I want one of the chaperones to come back and tell me. Then we'll have the aquarium security search for her. All right?"

Julie nodded. But before she could leave, Ms. Cook took her by the arm and said, "But don't you ever try to spin such fibs again, do you understand? If that's how you thought you could get out of calling your parents, you were wrong. I'm tempted to call them later and tell them about that ridiculous story you concocted. How do you think they'd like that?"

Julie shrugged. It didn't matter right now. All that mattered now was finding Millie and then rescuing Anne.

She walked calmly from the office, but once she was down the hall, she broke into a run.

Fifteen

Gambling, thought Anne. *That's the key.*

It seemed late, although it probably wasn't. Who could tell? Here in the dark, stinking hold of the *Sallie M.,* it always seemed to be midnight. Even with eyes adjusted to the darkness, figures were still shrouded in the grip of ebony shadows and charcoal shades.

Eternal night was here, a night whose morning would not bring the beautiful sun but the roar of waves taking them to a distant harbor and a life full of dread.

The people in the hold all seemed to be sleeping now, although it was hard to tell. How anyone could sleep or rest here was hard for Anne to imagine. Her own arms were cramped and aching so badly she felt like crying. Just having her arms held behind her had become a torture. She couldn't imagine what other true tortures faced these people if they were returned to their owners in the South. She had read in her history books about the treatment of slaves. But until now, the awful stories hadn't meant all that much to her.

Anne looked at the silhouette of Charles's body, curled up near the base of the ladder. What a hard life he had lived, having to endure working for Randolph

Ritchie. He was really a good person. Anne wondered what he would think if he was suddenly transported to her time, the late twentieth century, when there were no more slaves. She could just imagine the smile on his worn face.

Gambling is the key, she thought again. Randolph Ritchie loved to gamble. Charles had told her Ritchie always honored his bets, and although he usually won his wagers, he also would not back out if he lost.

Could she figure out a wager that could help free them all?

Suddenly the trapdoor slammed open.

"Charles!" shouted Randolph from above. Faint light filtered down the ladder, bringing dull bits of dust with it. Still, Anne couldn't tell what time it was. Probably six o'clock in the evening, or later.

"Charles!" Randolph shouted again.

Charles struggled up and grabbed the sides of the ladder. "What is it?" he called. His voice was groggy with fading sleep.

"Supper, what do you think? Are you as mindless as you are careless? Come up here and take this gruel down before I throw it into the harbor."

Charles climbed the ladder and disappeared through the hole.

Anne wondered how anyone ate with their hands and arms bound. Next to her, she could see the woman trying to straighten up a little.

"Did he say we was to get food now?" the woman asked.

"Yes," said Anne. "What's gruel?"

"Oh, honey," said the woman. "You haven't eaten 'til you've had gruel."

There was a gentle snicker from somewhere in the dark.

"What is it?" Anne asked.

"Food, honey, or what Randolph calls food. It's mashed grain mixed with water and heated just a little. I don't know where he gets his grain. Probably steals it from the shipments heading out of this place on the other boats."

"How long have you been with Randolph?" Anne asked.

The woman took a long breath. "I think it's been nearing a week now. Randolph knows if a slave gets to Pennsylvania, that's it. So he stays on the border with his dogs, watching, sniffing, ready. I was with my son, Juno. We got away from the farm in southeast Virginia and were doing real good. Found homes to stay in during the day, fine Quaker homes with fine Quaker folk who believe everyone should be free. But when we was nearing the border of Maryland, almost there, mind you, we could smell the freedom, Randolph and his dogs tracked us in the woods and brought us down."

Anne hesitated. She wondered if one of the silent figures in the dark was Juno. She asked, "And where is your son?"

The woman turned her face to Anne. Her voice was slow and controlled. "Dogs mauled him," she said.

"Randolph don't want to lose no slave, as you can see. But Juno fought the dogs and they mauled him. He died before we got into Baltimore."

Anne felt tears well up in her eyes. She didn't know the boy, but she knew that he had been loved and that his mother had done what she could to bring him to freedom.

"I'm so sorry," Anne whispered. "How old was he?"

"Seven."

"How can you stand it?" Anne said.

"Honey, life don't care if you hurt or not. It keeps on going, be you free or slave or old or young. Be you hurt or well or sick or spry. It's people caring for others that puts the good into life. If people don't care 'bout each other, then life don't, either. Freedom is what comes when people care 'bout each other. Without freedom, life is pain. Like Nettie over there said, freedom matters more than life."

"Freedom," came the hissing, insistent whispers from the corners and walls again.

Then Charles came down the ladder, the handle of a large bucket slung over one arm. He stepped onto the floor, lowered the pot, then turned the knob on the lantern, bringing the light up more fully. Anne winked in the unfamiliar brightness.

"Wake up," Charles called. "Food's here."

Anne watched as Charles took a large dipper from a hook on the wall and stirred it around inside the bucket.

"How do we eat?" she asked him. "Our hands are tied."

"You wait for me," he said. "I feed it to you."

"Not really."

Charles stopped stirring and looked at her. "Yes," he said, and she knew he was serious. "You sit until I bring the dipper to you. Four sips each. Randolph doesn't want the slaves to die of starvation, but he doesn't want anyone to have enough strength to fight."

Anne thought, then said, "I can help you, Charles. Untie me and I'll help you."

"I don't need help," Charles said. He lifted the dipper and let a stream of gruel pour back into the bucket. It was nasty-looking stuff, gray and lumpy.

"Randolph cut off your finger. I'm sure it hurts very badly. Let me do this for you. I promise I won't run."

Charles didn't say anything for a moment, then he said, "Not just my finger hurts. My whole hand. My whole arm."

"Then let me help you."

Charles rubbed his face. Then he said, "All right. But if you run away, even if you try, he will kill you. And then he might kill me, too."

"I know."

Charles moved to Anne. She leaned away from the wall as he used his good hand to work at the knot that bound her. A painful, tingling rush coursed through her wrists as the rope fell free.

"Thank you," Anne said.

"Don't thank me," Charles said. "It's probably a mistake."

Anne stood up. Her knees shook madly. She rubbed her hands and wrists and flexed her fingers. "Sit down and rest, Charles. I'll feed the people."

Charles slid to the floor at the bottom of the ladder. He pointed to the lantern. "Take that. You'll need it."

Anne picked up the lantern and slipped the handle onto her elbow. She lifted the bucket with the dipper. It was quite heavy. She walked awkwardly to the woman who had been beside her.

"Do you want some?" she asked timidly.

"My belly is sore with being empty," said the woman. "Give me what I can have."

"Four sips?"

The woman nodded.

Anne stepped closer. As the lantern swayed on her elbow, and the light crossed the woman's face at close range, Anne could see long scabby marks on her cheeks. They looked like lash marks, whip marks. Perhaps it had been done by her master in Virginia. Perhaps it had been done by Randolph Ritchie. The woman saw Anne staring. She said, "Be brave, my girl." Then she closed her eyes and opened her mouth.

Anne gave her, one at a time, four dippers full of the lumpy, gray liquid.

Then, she went on to the next person.

Sixteen

Now, thought Julie as she sat on a bench in a small outdoor amphitheater near the shops of Harborplace, *the buses are gone. Ms. Cook is busy with Jerry. They won't realize I changed the note for a long time. And before they do, I have to find Millie.*

Julie had taken Ms. Cook's note to the chaperones at the buses, but not before she had changed it. She'd scratched out the line about Anne's being missing, and she had added a P.S. It had said, "Julie is coming back to the aquarium to work this out with Jerry and me. Go on without her."

The handwriting looked something like Ms. Cook's, although the pen Julie had had in her pocket was filled with blue ink, and Ms. Cook had written in black. Luckily, the chaperone, a student teacher named Miss Nennson, didn't seem to notice or to care, especially when Julie had made herself look as if she didn't want to have to go back to the aquarium.

"Should have been more careful," Miss Nennson had said. "Tell Ms. Cook I've got everything covered and she won't have to worry."

Julie had nodded. And the buses had rolled off, swallowed into the traffic of busy downtown Baltimore.

Julie had then run back to the harbor.

A little boy sat down beside Julie and grinned up at her. He had an ice-cream cone in his hand and a smudge of chocolate ice cream on his face. Normally, Julie would have talked to the boy, but right now, she didn't have time to be friendly. She had to think.

"Hi," said the boy.

"Hi," said Julie. She turned away from the boy and looked out across the water. A short way down the shore, still moored to the pier, was the tourist boat. There was no vision there. No sighting of an old sailing ship and ghostly people taking Anne onto the deck. But Julie knew she hadn't been imagining it.

"Hi," said the boy again. Julie continued to ignore him and look at the tourist boat. Millie had been dressed like someone from that ghost time, about mid-nineteenth-century, Julie guessed. Had she somehow come to *this* time, and Anne had taken Millie's place?

Where *was* Millie? If she had gone far, it would be almost impossible to find her. This city was so big. There were so many people.

"Hi," said the little boy beside Julie.

Irritated, Julie turned and looked at him with a frown. "Where are your parents?" she demanded.

The little boy grinned, then pointed toward a small crowd around an umbrella-covered ice-cream stand. The mother and father were talking and waiting for their own cones, seemingly not concerned with their little boy.

"You'd better go on back to them," Julie said. "They'll wonder where you are." *Although they don't seem to be wondering very much,* she thought.

The boy smiled and shook his head.

"I'm busy," said Julie.

"There's a funny lady there," said the boy, and he pointed toward the water.

Julie said, "Go back to your parents. It's dangerous to . . ." And then she stopped. "What did you say?"

The boy took a lick of his cone. Some of the chocolate dripped to his lap and he rubbed at it, only making the stain on his pants worse. "There's a funny lady down there. She made me laugh."

Julie's heart began to beat faster. "A funny lady? What did she look like?"

The boy sniffed and licked ice cream off the back of his hand. He said, "Funny clothes. All tore up. She's hiding."

Julie sat forward. She wanted to grab the boy and make him take her where he'd seen the funny lady, but she knew she could be in big trouble if she even touched the child.

"Where?" she said slowly. "Where did you see the funny lady hiding?"

"Under there." The boy pointed with the ice-cream cone toward a small pier jutting out just below the flat stage of the amphitheater. No boats were moored to it. A cluster of herring gulls sat on the boards, looking around, occasionally flapping their wings at each other.

"Under the pier?"

The boy said, "I said 'hi' to her and she crawled away real far up under there. She don't got no shoes on!" He laughed again. "It's too cold for no shoes!"

"Joey!" Julie turned to see the parents rushing over to the bench seat, their ice-cream cones wobbling, their faces pinched with worry. As they reached the boy, they gave Julie a nervous glance. "Joey, you wandered away! You know you're supposed to stay beside us at all times. You don't talk to people you don't know!"

Joey didn't seem concerned. "A funny lady is hiding and she don't have no shoes!" he said with a smile.

The mother grabbed the little boy's hand and pulled him up. He gasped as his ice-cream cone fell to the ground.

"Mama!" he cried.

"Come with us," the father said. "If we have to hold your hand the rest of the evening, we'll do it, young man!"

And they were gone.

The boy had said a funny lady was hiding under the pier. Julie stood up, biting her lower lip.

Millie?

Julie ran along the bench and out of the amphitheater. She excused herself as she passed between a couple throwing bread crumbs to gulls, and raced down to the pier.

Out in the harbor, a large ship carrying unknown cargo and heading to an unknown destination passed, moving slowly and almost silently along the near-black water. Julie stood at the front of the pier and looked down through the cracks in the wood planks.

She cleared her throat. "Millie?"

There was no sound except for the tourists behind her and the squawking gulls at the end of the pier who had turned to stare at her.

"Millie? Are you down there?"

Again, there was no answer.

Julie went to the side of the pier and glanced over. There was about four feet of sandy soil before the water's edge. Joey must have gotten away from his parents long enough to jump down there and explore. That's when he'd seen the funny lady.

What if it wasn't Millie? What if it was an insane woman with a knife or gun?

Gritting her teeth, Julie held on to one of the pier's posts and let herself slide down to the wet harbor shore.

She bent down and looked beneath the pier. It was hard to see. The sun was setting in the west to her right, and the shadow beneath the pier was as thick as tar. She squinted, then knelt in the sand. Wetness spread quickly on the knees of her jeans.

"Millie, are you under there?"

There was a soft shuffling sound. Then, there was a cough.

"Millie?"

Julie moved forward on her knees into the darkness beneath the pier. The soaked, sandy ground was uneven and awkward, and she kept her hands out beside her so she wouldn't fall over. Although she loved aquatic animals, she hoped she wouldn't come down on top of a crab.

"Millie?" she said again, and then a soft voice said, "Yes?"

Julie's chest heaved a sigh of relief. The girl was here, hiding. No wonder, though. If Julie had found herself in a future time, she would look for a place to hide, too.

Stopping for a moment, Julie let her eyes adjust. There, with her back against the wall of hard-packed dirt, was Millie. Her knees were drawn up, her bare feet covered with sand past her ankles. She held her wounded wrist protectively to her chest.

"Millie, I'm so glad I've found you. We need to talk."

Millie said, "I don't know what to say to you. I don't know what is happening, or where I am."

Julie wanted to get closer to Millie, but was afraid she would scare the girl again and that she would run away once more. So she sat on the wet sand facing Millie.

"My friend, Anne, is missing," she began. "I can't explain how or why, but I think you are the key. Earlier, I didn't believe what you were telling me. You said things about slavery and running away to freedom in the North. It sounded so crazy. But now, I think you are the only one to help me find my friend and bring her back to safety."

Millie said, "I'm missing, too."

"Yes," said Julie. "That's what I'm getting to. Somehow, I think you and she switched places."

"Switched places?"

Julie clenched her fists, but tried to stay calm. Her heart thumped painfully, thinking again of what Anne must be going through.

"You said you were running north," Julie said. "To get to freedom. You said you were running away from a catcher. What year was that?"

"Year?" asked Millie. "What number of the year?"

"Yes."

"Why, it is 1849. Don't you know that? I have no learning, but even I know that."

1849, thought Julie. She was right when she'd thought Millie's clothes looked as if they were from the nineteenth-century. "Tell me, where were you when you found yourself in the museum?"

In the shadows, Millie blinked, confused.

"When you found yourself on the floor, and you first saw me?" Julie pressed. "Where were you before you came here?"

"I was on a pier," Millie said. "Randolph Ritchie's boy had me by the arms. But I wasn't tied yet. My arm hurt so bad. The boy said he was going to put me on the ship. He was going to put me down in the hold and take me back to Lawton Plantation in South Carolina." Millie's voice cracked, and she took a gasping breath. It sounded as though she was going to cry.

"Millie, take the bandanna off your head."

"Why?"

"Please, I can at least make a sling for your wrist."

Millie shook her head.

"Why not?"

"My hair," Millie said, then stopped.

"What about your hair?"

"It's cut off," Millie said.

Julie was confused. "Short hair is cute," she said. "Let me bind up your wrist so it won't hurt so bad."

Millie shook her head.

"All right," Julie said with frustration. "But think, please. What happened right before you came here? Did something strange happen? Something must have. Think. Try to remember."

"I don't remember."

"It's important."

"I don't remember."

"Please try, Millie."

Millie said nothing.

"Then come with me," said Julie. She looked back at the girl in the shadows. "I want to show you the boat where I saw the image. Maybe the two of us can figure out what happened and we can get Anne back."

Millie was silent, then she said, "If your friend comes back to you, will I go back?"

Julie thought, *I don't know. Millie, Anne has to come back to this time. I can't let her stay where she is. But I don't want you in danger, either. I don't know what will happen to you.*

"Come on," Julie said, holding out her hand to the girl, ignoring Millie's question.

Seventeen

Anne dropped the empty bucket beside Charles.

"Everyone's fed," she said. "I guess you have to take the bucket back up to Randolph."

Charles sat, the hand with its finger stump in his pocket.

"No, he won't think about it again until morning, when the people down here start moaning for water. He uses the same bucket for water and food."

"He's insane."

"Maybe." Charles looked up at Anne. He looked very tired. "I have to tie your hands back up."

Anne sat on the filthy floor beside the boy. She said, "No, you don't. Don't you think you can trust me by now?"

"You knocked me in the harbor earlier. I can't swim. I know you'd do what you could to get away from us."

"I *didn't* knock you in the water. I told you that already."

Charles rubbed his neck slowly. The lantern light was even paler now, the wick inside down to a nub. "I was lucky that I was close enough to the pier to grab hold and pull myself up from the water. Then Ritchie was there beside me, and you were there by the barrels on the shore. You had to have knocked me in the water to save the runaway."

Anne put her hands over her eyes. He would never believe her. "I didn't do anything like that. But it doesn't matter if you believe me or not. Don't tie my hands. Please."

Charles tilted his head slightly. "You telling me if I don't tie you you won't run? You promise that if you get the chance, you won't run away?"

Anne thought about that. If the chance came to get away, she knew she would. Could she promise not to run, only to run when the opportunity came?

She said, "I promise for now not to run away."

"How long is 'for now'?"

Anne shrugged. "For now. I don't know more. But Charles, I have to get home."

"I'd like to go home someday."

"Where is home, Charles?"

"I grew up just west of Baltimore. Besides my father, I've got a mother and two little brothers. But as I told you, they are very poor. My father is a dockman at the train station they built the year I was born, 1833. My father loves trains. I remember when I was little going to see the *Tom Thumb* taking off out of Baltimore. What a sight it was! All smoke and noise and power. I think my father likes the idea of hopping on a locomotive and heading west for adventure." Charles was almost smiling now, lost in his memories.

"I've never ridden on a train," said Anne.

"Well," said Charles, "how many people have, I ask you? It's such a new thing. So many things come into the city now to be shipped out. Tobacco, grains. This city has grown so big."

"You miss your family?"

"Do you think I don't?" Charles asked.

"I bet you're really mad at your dad for giving you to Randolph," Anne said quietly.

Charles was silent for a minute. Then he said, "Mad? Maybe I am, or maybe I was. No longer. We do what we must. And children have been sold for less, you know. My father was sad but said nothing except for me to do my job and do it well. If it was a smithing job, or a dockman's job, I would do it well, as he asked. I don't think he knows what it is to be a slave catcher. We never talked about slavery in our family. There was no need to. We weren't planters. We did our own chores and labor. We saw slaves on errands in town with their masters. We thought little of it. But now . . ." Charles paused. "Now, I've seen it for what it really is. God help us."

Anne had an itch on her chin. She rubbed her face into her shoulder to ease it. "When you are free from Ritchie, what do you want to do?"

"I'll probably work at the station with my father. That will be a wonderful day. We will work together. I will never speak of my time with Ritchie." Charles shook his head sadly. "I will certainly not follow in Ritchie's footsteps, 'though I've learned his trade well. Maybe one day no one will have to."

"It's going to get worse before it gets better," said Anne. She remembered a little bit of the history she'd studied; suddenly it was all too painfully real. "In 1850, in a year from now, there is going to be a new law passed. It's called the Fugitive Slave Law. Even runaways who get to the North can be brought back if a slave catcher finds them. They will only be safe in Canada."

Charles narrowed his eyes. "How do you know?"

"I know," said Anne.

"Do you think it will ever end?"

Anne said, "It will. Not many more years ahead. I promise." *If Randolph lets you live that long,* Anne thought sadly.

They sat quietly for a few minutes, and then Anne realized Charles had fallen asleep. She looked at the lantern, burning dimly. Then she looked back into the shadows, where the captured runaways were. Most, it seemed, were asleep.

Gambling is the key, she thought. But she couldn't think of anything to gamble with, and if she lost to Randolph Ritchie, what would that mean?

Eighteen

"Tell me about your family," said Julie. She and Millie were walking along the side of the harbor, moving toward the moored tourist boat where Julie had seen the vision of Anne. Julie had hold of Millie's elbow, and every few seconds, it felt as if the girl would bolt from fear. And so, Julie held the cloth of her sleeve tightly and spoke in soft tones.

Millie, barefoot, didn't seem to notice the sharp stone and shells that lay along the harbor shore. Her arm, though, still clearly gave her great pain. Julie wished she could do something about it, but didn't know what.

"My mama is sold off," Millie said quietly. "Sold off to the turpentine woods in Georgia. A bad place, they say, worse than Lawton Plantation. Mama give the Missus a hard time about her beating me when I had an infected foot and couldn't work, so they sold her down to Georgia. Turpentine overseers'll cut your foot off if you even look like you want to run. They beat a man or woman to death for having a scowl. People get sick in the heat, and there is lots of dying from the sickness."

"That's terrible," said Julie. She knew she had ancestors who had been slaves, but actually to speak to someone who had experienced the horrors was almost too much to imagine. If she had lived in 1849, she would have tried to run away, too.

"I have little sisters, three of them," said Millie. "I want to be free, to go be with my cousins in New York and earn money to buy their freedom."

"That's a wonderful idea."

"I'm going to own my own land. I'm going to change my name and hold my head up proud. I can do it. I know I can. That man caught me, but I'm not caught any longer. I can get to Pennsylvania; I know it."

Julie said, "I know you'll make it, Millie." *If we get you back to your time,* she thought. *And when you do get back, I hope you escape the catcher and make it to freedom.* Julie's head spun. Too many things to think about, most of them unbelievable. They reached the end of the tourist boat's pier. Behind them, the sun had set, and lights had begun to come on all over Harborplace, making a cheery, bright backdrop to a frightening situation.

Nineteen

Down in the hold, Anne sat watching as Charles slept. She wanted to take everyone with her, she wanted to free all the tied people and take them and Charles back with her to *her* Baltimore, where they would be safe and would never again be in danger because of slavery. Where they could start new lives.

But she knew that would be impossible.

Only *she* had crossed over to the past. Only *she* could cross back. If she tried to take the slaves or Charles with her, it would be certain death for them.

What a terrible choice, to go without them. Toby, the nameless ten-year-old girl, the kind woman who talked about the death of her son, Juno. None of them deserved to be here. No one deserved this inhumanity. But there was nothing she could do.

Or was there?

There had been no sound above deck for quite a while. Randolph, as much whiskey as he had drunk, was most likely passed out at long last in his cabin. Anne knew she had more courage than Charles, but only because he had been beaten down so often that he was afraid to attempt something dangerous.

If she went up the ladder and found Randolph passed out, could she get away then?

If he was passed out, could she sneak the runaways from the hold and let them escape into the dark streets of Baltimore? Maybe she couldn't take them with her to her own time, but would they have a fair chance at freedom if she untied them and they escaped into the Baltimore of 1849?

The thoughts made her feel dizzy. Never in her life had she had such responsibility hanging over her head. Yes, she baby-sat her cousin, but making sure a toddler didn't play with sharp objects and went to bed on time was nothing compared to this. This truly was a life-and-death situation.

She looked at the lantern. If she took it up, the light, even as bare as it was, might be enough to catch Ritchie's attention.

Anne grabbed both sides of the ladder and climbed up to the deck of the boat. Carefully, she pushed against the trapdoor, and it lifted up. She grasped it and eased it over so that it wouldn't thump on the wood of the deck. Then she crawled out into the fresh air and the moonlight.

Taking a deep breath, Anne stood up and looked around. It was very dark now. There were very few lights along the shore, not like the harbor in her own time. She remembered bright lights and happy people and colorful boats cruising up and down the waterway. Here it looked as if someone had gone down the shoreline and blown all the lights out as if they were birthday candles.

Heart pounding, Anne tiptoed to the door of Randolph Ritchie's cabin and pressed her ear to the wood. She listened.

The only sound from inside the room was that of rough snoring and coughing. The man was definitely passed out. He would probably remain that way until morning, when he would pull up the anchor and sail into the Chesapeake Bay and then the Atlantic Ocean.

It was time to act. Now or never. She didn't know exactly how she was going to get back to her own time, but she knew it wouldn't be by staying on this ship. She also knew the slaves only had one chance, and that chance was her. Quietly, Anne ran back to the trapdoor and slid down the ladder.

Charles was still asleep, although he had turned over on his side. Carefully, Anne bent over and looked to see if he might have something with which she could cut the slaves' ropes. There was a pale glint from the pocket of his vest. She slowly reached and pulled the object out. It was a dull knife, like the ones the men had used in the tavern for eating. Charles must have stolen it. Anne couldn't imagine it would be much of a weapon. Maybe he wanted to sell it for a little money.

"I said I wouldn't run for now," she whispered. "But that now is gone. *This* now is different. I have to do this. I hope it doesn't put you in danger, Charles."

Holding the knife to her side, she crept to Juno's mother. As she reached out for the rope, the woman awoke with a start. Her eyes flashed wide open, easy to see even in the dim light.

"What . . ." the woman began.

"Ritchie is asleep," said Anne quietly. "Drunk to the world. I am going to loosen all of you, and then you can run off the ship before he wakes up."

The woman glanced at Charles. "He'll beat the boy to death if we get away."

"As soon as you are all untied, I'm going to waken Charles. He can run away, too. He hates working for Randolph Ritchie. Baltimore is a big city; I mean, I'm pretty sure it's a big city. It is in my time. There are lots of places to hide during the day. And tomorrow night, you can head north."

As the woman's arms came free from behind her, and her ankles were cut loose, she reached out and took Anne's face in her hands. She looked back at the others, who seemed to be stirring awake. "Bless you, child."

"Go now," said Anne. "The sooner, the better."

"Bless you," the woman repeated. "But I'll wait for the others. We may all go north our own way once we're off this ship, but I want to know at least we all got off it in the first place."

"That's taking a big chance."

"Maybe," said the woman. "But I'll risk it."

Anne looked at her for a moment, then said, "I understand."

Together, Anne and the woman moved silently from person to person, Anne slicing at the ropes with the dull knife, the woman untying the knots that were not so tight. The runaways blinked at them as they worked, listening to the whispered explanation of what was going on, nodding with weary excitement at the word "freedom."

Then Anne stopped at Toby, the old man who had danced to the rhythm of the bullets on the upper deck. He seemed to be still asleep. She shook his bony shoulder.

"Toby," she whispered. "Toby, it's time to get away."

Toby didn't move.

Anne bent closer and shook him again.

"Toby, please wake up. You can get away if you go now!"

Toby didn't open his eyes, and he still didn't move. The woman came over to Anne and knelt beside her. After a moment, she said, "Toby's gone to another freedom. Toby's free of this world."

Anne, realizing what she meant, said, "Oh, no, please."

The woman nodded, taking a shaky breath that sounded as if it was holding back tears. "Yes. Toby's never going to have ropes nor chains no more. No catcher ever going to have dogs after him. He'll have shoes and a crown and joy forevermore."

Anne felt her own eyes rim with tears. The woman touched her arm and said, "We cry in our hearts. But we can't cry aloud. Not now, anyway. Now we must take this chance to run. Toby would want us to run."

Anne nodded. She and the woman moved to the next runaway.

It only took a few minutes to cut all the ropes. Anne had counted, and there were seventeen people altogether. As she and the woman undid the rope of the last captive, Anne thought, *This is going to work! We're going to get away!*

The slaves stood, rubbing aching arms and legs. Anne held her finger up to her lips and motioned for them to go quietly to the ladder.

The nameless little girl was hastened to the front of the line by the others. A man stood behind her as she took the first few rungs of the ladder, holding out his arms behind her in case she didn't have the strength to climb. Anne stood beside the ladder, her chest still tight with fear, but her mind spinning with happiness knowing that these people would be free.

And then Charles gasped. Anne looked down at him. His eyes were open, and he was staring up at her with dread.

"No, don't let them get away," he pleaded.

Twenty

"I saw my friend here," Julie said. "She was climbing onto a strange ship, not like the one you see there. It was like a ghost, like an image of some sort. But the girl I saw climbing the gangplank was Anne, I'm certain of it."

Millie said nothing. She just stared out at the tourist ship.

"I need you to tell me everything that happened right before you found yourself here. I mean *everything*. What you saw, what you heard, even what you smelled. Please. I need anything you can tell me so I can somehow help Anne."

Millie said, "I was going on a ship to go back south. Randolph and his dogs caught me. I fell on my arm and my wrist broke."

"Yes," said Julie. "You told me that. I need details about what happened on the plank."

"I don't remember."

Julie reached out for Millie's arm. She took it gently but firmly. "Please, please think."

Millie closed her eyes. Her face drew up. "The boy didn't like it," she said finally.

"The boy?"

"The boy who held me and was taking me onto the ship. Ritchie was on the shore. His dogs were already in the cabin, and he was on his way to the tavern. He stopped because a bootstrap broke. He was cursing. The boy hadn't taken me onto the deck yet because . . ." Millie stopped. Her eyes opened. She looked angry, embarrassed.

"Because what?"

"Because Ritchie told him not to bring me on board until he'd checked my head for lice. I don't have lice. I never did. But he thought I was dirty. He thinks all slaves are dirty."

Julie looked again at the bandanna on Millie's head. "What did he do?"

Millie bit her lip. "Ritchie made the boy shave my head with his knife. Cut my hair all off. There wasn't any lice. Ritchie just told the boy to do it because he thought it was funny." Millie looked straight at Julie then. "I had a bandanna around my neck. After he shaved my head, the boy let me put it on. Ritchie was messing around with his boot and would have made me take it off if he'd seen. Then we walked up the plank, and then"—Millie stopped and took a deep breath—"then I felt myself falling and opened my eyes in that room with the fish."

"Did you say anything before you woke up here?"

"No. I was just thinking, 'Lord, let there be a day when slavery is no more.' "

Julie reached up and gently touched the brown bandanna. "Millie, trust me, all right? I know you don't have lice. I don't care that your hair is gone. Trust me."

Millie closed her eyes, and nodded.

Julie slid the bandanna from the girl's head. The hair was indeed gone, shaved close in some spots, not so close in others. It didn't matter. Julie unwound the cloth and made a small triangular sling. "Millie," she said.

Millie opened her eyes.

"This will help hold your wrist in place," she said. She put it around the wrist, carefully pulled the wrist up high, close to Millie's throat, then tied the cloth around the girl's neck. "Keeping it still will ease the pain a little."

"Thank you," Millie said.

"I want you to go with me onto that boat," Julie explained. "Maybe there we'll see a vision of Anne again. Maybe then I can figure out how to help her."

Millie hesitated, then nodded. Julie looked back over her shoulder. No one was watching them. Then she looked at the sign on the chain across the plank to the tourist boat. "Closed Until Our Moonlight Trip," the sign still read. "Open 9:30 P.M." There was time to get on, look around, and call for Anne.

Quickly, Julie led Millie down the pier and under the chain. The two girls jumped down onto the first deck of the tourist boat. Julie looked over her shoulder toward the shore.

"Nobody saw us," she said.

"No," said Millie.

"Come on, then."

Julie walked around the far side of the boat to a door that led inside the enclosed passenger area. She tried the door and it opened with a squeak. She and Millie went inside.

Colorful plastic chairs sat in rows, bolted to the floor and facing the long plate glass windows on either side of the boat. Julie assumed that this way, if it was cold, people could sit down here and watch the scenery. If it was warm, she supposed, they could sit on the upper deck, where there was no roof and they could get the breeze off the harbor. One day, she thought, she might come back here and take this tour. She would watch the water for signs of fish and other aquatic life. She would enjoy the movement of the boat as little waves splashed against its sides and think about the time when she would be a marine biologist.

But that was some other day.

Some other time.

She would never again be able to think of fish and her dreams if she couldn't save Anne.

Millie sat carefully on one of the plastic seats. Her hand ran over the surface with careful amazement. "Never sat on nothing like this before," she said.

Julie almost felt herself smile.

And then it began again. The room in which she stood began to shimmer, and she grabbed for the back of a chair so she wouldn't lose her balance. She gasped.

Millie said sharply, "What's wrong?"

"It's happening," Julie managed.

"What?"

"Just wait, I'll tell you."

The room with the plastic chairs flickered, and something else was there, lying over the scene once more like a piece of faint film. Julie could see the old ship she'd seen before, but this time, she was standing on it. There was a raised end with a steering wheel. She turned carefully to look at the other end and saw a small, boxy room like a shed. And in the center of the deck, there was a trapdoor.

"I see an old ship," Julie made herself say. "Not long, but with sails tied up. There is a steering wheel, and a cabin on the other end. I don't see anyone."

"Might be the *Sallie M.*," said Millie.

"*Sallie M.?*"

"Randolph Ritchie's boat."

Julie felt ice forming in her veins. Randolph Ritchie's boat. *Anne,* she thought. *Where are you?*

Through the vision of the old ship, Julie could see Millie stand up and take her by the arm. "You seeing the *Sallie M.?* God help us!"

"It's only a vision," Julie said. "Don't be afraid."

As Julie looked around the deck of the sailing ship, movement caught her eye. She glanced down. The trapdoor was pushing open, falling back and hitting the floor, leaving a black, square hole in the middle of the deck.

Suddenly, a hand reached up through the hole, grabbing at air, seeming to grab for freedom.

Julie stumbled backward, away from the ghostly,

grasping fingers. And she bumped into something solid, something that moved. She whipped around.

The vision of the old sailing ship vanished.

There, standing with a flashlight, pistol, and snarling Doberman pinscher, was a man in security guard clothing.

"Don't move!" he shouted, grabbing Julie's arm forcefully. "You have no right to be here!"

Twenty-one

"We have to, Charles," Anne whispered urgently. "Randolph's asleep, and if we don't run away now, we'll never have the chance again."

"He'll find out!"

"He won't. It's wrong not to try to get away. If we don't, that's letting evil win!"

The girl on the ladder had paused, and she looked back down, waiting to see if she could go on. Both Anne and the man behind her whispered at the same time, "Go!"

The girl scrambled up the ladder.

Others began to file after, moving up the ladder as silently as feathers on the wind.

Charles grabbed Anne by the arms. "What will happen to us? To me? To you? Randolph doesn't let people get away, ever! He'll have us back, I know it! Call the runaways down and we'll pretend this never happened!"

"No!" said Anne. "And be quiet or you'll ruin it. Charles, you'll go, too. We'll all go. We'll be safe. But it's now or never."

Other runaways moved quietly to the bottom of the
ladder and climbed up.

Charles let go of Anne. He stared without speaking
as the last of the runaways made it to the ladder and
began to climb. Then he squinted into the far corner.
"There's still someone back there," he said, with resignation in his voice. "If some go, all must go."

"It's Toby," Anne said softly. "He's dead."

Charles sighed. "I'm sorry to hear it. I'm sorry I've
ever been part of this." He looked up the ladder. The
last slave was gone through the trapdoor opening. Then
he held his hand out, palm up.

"After you," he said.

Anne grabbed the ladder and climbed quickly to the
square hole above her head. She felt the ladder tremble
a little as Charles began to climb up behind her.

As she pulled herself through the opening and onto
the deck, she saw the last of the slaves climb over the
side of the deck and onto the gangplank. She stood,
and strained to see in the night. A silent line of people,
now on the shore, ran toward the buildings, holding
low.

"Yes," Anne whispered. "Yes, they got away!" She
turned and held out her hand to help Charles as his
head appeared in the opening of the trapdoor hole.

Charles took her hand and climbed onto the deck.
His eyes were huge with fear, but his jaw was set with
determination.

He lifted the trapdoor and shut it gently back over
the hole.

"They all got off the boat," he said softly to Anne, a note of amazement in his voice.

"Yes," said Anne. "And now we must hurry, too."

"Before we do," Charles said. "I want to thank you. We'll probably each go our own way, and will never see each other again. Thank you for saving our lives." And then, to Anne's surprise, he leaned over and gave her a hug.

She shut her eyes for a moment. She hoped Charles would find a new life, a new . . .

"If lightning struck me, I'd be no more fried!"

Anne whipped about and Charles stumbled backward.

Randolph Ritchie stood just outside his cabin door, suspenders drooping, his unsheathed sword in his hand.

"Oh, my God!" cried Charles.

"You best be praying!" Randolph bellowed. "Because you'll have no sympathy from me!" And taking heavy steps, he strode boldly toward Anne and Charles.

Twenty-two

"You wait right here," said the security guard as he pushed Julie and Millie into the rest room at the corner of the tourist boat's lower deck. Before he shut the door, he pulled a walkie-talkie from a leather pocket at his waist. "I see you're only young girls, but I can't take chances. This is my job, you see, and I'm to report anyone on these boats without permission. There has been quite a bit of vandalism recently."

Julie said nothing. Millie, eyes wide, said nothing. The guard then shut the rest room door, leaving the two girls standing alone in the middle of the floor.

Through the closed door, Julie could hear the man speaking to someone on the other end of the walkie-talkie.

"What are we going to do?" Millie said.

"I don't know," Julie answered. "I really don't. There isn't a window in here. If there was, we could jump out into the water."

"I can't swim," Millie cried. "There are dangerous animals in harbor water!"

"I swim well. I could help you if we had to go into

the water," said Julie. "And I know a lot about aquatic animals. There's nothing dangerous in there, I'm sure."

Millie turned around slowly. Seeing the reflection of herself in the mirror over the sink, she quickly looked away.

"Millie, please," Julie begged. "We don't have much time. Tell me what happened the *exact* second you fell."

Millie shook her head.

"Millie, *please!*"

Millie's eyes welled up and tears fell. "I only was saying 'slavery must be no more.' I've told you that. I can't think of anything else!"

"I'm sorry," said Julie. "But . . ."

Another scene began to take shape and form inside the tiny bathroom. Julie suddenly could see the inside of another small room, with a bed and a small table. A man, the one she had seen with the boots and dirty white shirt, stood just inside the door. His face was twisted in a terrible grin, and he was uncoiling a long black whip. Julie shifted her eyes and saw another rippling image in the corner of the ghost room. She saw Anne, hands over her face, cowering in fear.

Twenty-three

Randolph Ritchie uncoiled his whip, then snapped it in the air above Anne's head.

"Never," he said slowly, his voice hissing out through his teeth like the warning sound of a poisonous snake, "never has anyone made me as angry as I am now." He snapped the whip again; it whistled close by Anne's ear. "Never has a worthless gypsy and a bunch of slaves gotten away from me."

Anne tried to press her body more tightly into the corner. Her mind spun, trying to grasp a way out of this. At this moment, Charles was tied to the center beam on the boat's deck; she knew Randolph meant to beat him when he was through with her. He would probably beat her to death, and then do the same to Charles.

"You lost me my earnings for a whole month," Randolph said. He stepped closer to Anne. He ran his fingers up and down the whip, caressing it the way someone would stroke a pet dog. "A month of chasing, a month of running through the rough land. A month of docking fees for the *Sallie M.*, a month of Charles's time wasted."

"I . . ." Anne began. Was she going to tell him she was sorry? She wasn't. Was she going to try to explain? He would never understand. Was she going to beg for her life and that of Charles?

"What?" demanded Randolph, thrusting his face so close to Anne's that she could almost count the hairs of his dirty beard.

"I'd like to make a wager," she said.

Randolph stood back, his eyes wide in amazement. He put his hands on his hips. The long end of the whip curled about his boots. "A wager?" he demanded. "You, a gypsy girl, want to make a wager with me? That's insane, you little pig!"

"Maybe so, but I want to make a bet with you," said Anne.

The man smiled a terrible smile. "You must know I never walk from a wager," he said. "And you must also know my reputation for never going back on the wager, win or lose."

"I know," said Anne. "I've seen you bet on several things already. The waitress in the tavern. The bet that Toby could dance. I know you didn't go back on those."

"Then you also must know," Randolph said, his smile fading and a twitching frown taking its place, "that I rarely lose a wager. And I've never lost a wager to a stinking gypsy. I've never lost to a woman or a gypsy or a slave. But thinking of it now, I can't remember ever making a bet with a woman or gypsy or slave before."

Anne took a breath. "Do you accept my wager or are you going to walk away from it?"

Randolph's eyes flashed. "You silly pig! I'll eat your wager and when I'm through with you, the fish will have you for dinner! I'll have your bet and you'll wish you'd never thought of such a scheme!"

"The wager will have to be done outside on the deck," Anne said. "We'll need more room."

"What is it?" Randolph asked. "Hand-to-hand combat?"

Anne shook her head. "No, but we must be out on the deck."

Randolph gripped the whip handle tightly, then turned and yanked open the cabin door. He stepped back, waiting for Anne to go out first. As Anne walked through the door into the fresh air and the pale moonlight, she thought frantically. She didn't know what she was going to bet. She had no idea of what to wager Randolph. All she knew was that if she'd stayed in that cabin longer with the man, she was going to be killed.

His shirt torn from his body and his arms lashed behind him to the center beam, Charles watched Anne and Randolph as they came out of the cabin. He said nothing, but Anne could read terror in his eyes.

I've got to think of something! Anne's mind screamed. *I have to come up with a bet I can win! Gambling is the key if I can only think of something!*

"Well," said Randolph. "Tell me now what you are going to bet me?"

"First, let's come up with the stakes," said Anne.

"It doesn't work that way, pig," said Randolph. "We don't discuss stakes until we see what it is that will be tested. Do you want to have a shooting match? Do you want to throw knives? Do you want to see who can flick hairs from Charles's head without cutting his scalp?"

Anne looked at Charles. He was looking at the deck. She knew it was her fault he was in such danger now.

"You were stalling me!" Randolph said suddenly. "You have no bet! You only thought it would stall me and what I have planned for you! If you don't tell me the wager now, I'll cut off another of Charles's fingers and then take the whip to him. When I'm through with him, it will be your turn at the post!"

And then Anne knew what she was going to bet. She remembered an old trick she'd learned in sixth grade. A rush of relief flowed through her body and she began to shake with excitement. This was a bet she could win; she knew it!

"I do have a bet," she said.

Randolph said, "And what is that?"

"I bet I can make nine sticks into ten without breaking a one."

"That's because you're a gypsy!" barked Randolph. "You can bewitch sticks!"

"No," said Anne. "I can do it and you'll see there is no magic at all. You can do it. Anyone can do it."

Randolph seemed to consider her words. He crossed his arms and stared at Anne. "No magic at all. If there is magic, I'll kill you."

"No magic," Anne repeated.

"Hmmm," said Randolph.

"Is it a bet, then?" asked Anne.

"No one can make nine sticks into ten without breaking one," said Randolph, "It's a wager." He held out one hand to Anne as if he were going to shake hers, then, as if realizing he was offering to shake the hand of a gypsy, he crossed his arms again.

"Now we'll decide on the stakes," Anne said. "Freedom for Charles and me if I win."

"Ha!" Randolph laughed. "I will wager that because I know you can't win the bet. And if *I* win, which I most surely will, you and Charles will scour the city of Baltimore with me to find as many runaways as we can. We will bring them back here. Then, I will shoot both of you."

"It's a wager," said Anne.

Randolph lifted the lantern from beside the cabin door. "I'll take you to shore to find the sticks," he said, "then we will bring them back here. You'll show me your ridiculous bet."

As Randolph and Anne stepped over the side of the boat to the gangplank, Anne looked back at Charles. His eyes were closed as if he knew Anne didn't have a chance of winning the bet.

Don't worry, she thought. *We'll be free very soon!*

Twenty-four

"I saw Anne!" said Julie as the vision of her friend in the corner of the room and the man with the whip faded. "I saw her and she's going to be hurt, maybe killed!"

Millie gasped. "What can we do?"

"We have to get out of this bathroom first," said Julie. "I can't think in here. We have to get out!"

Millie began to moan and groan loudly. She bent over and held her stomach with her free hand.

"What are you doing?" Julie asked.

"Pretending that I am sick," Millie whispered. "The man may come in and we can get out." Then she began to groan more loudly.

Julie pounded on the bathroom door. "My friend's really sick!" she called. "She's bent over and her stomach hurts! I think her heart hurts! I don't know what's the matter with her! Don't leave us in here. She might die! Please, help us!"

Through the door and over the loud wails of Millie, Julie could hear the guard say, "Oh, this is just great!" Then she heard the doorknob rattle, and she stepped back, to let him in.

The door opened with a whoosh, and Julie and Millie were ready. Julie knocked the guard against the wall and grabbed the walkie-talkie from his hand. Millie grabbed the leash of the snarling black dog and pulled so hard that the dog went skidding up under the sink, his claws clacking and scrambling on the tile floor. Then, before the dog or guard could regain their footing, Julie and Millie dashed from the bathroom door, slammed the door shut, and leaned against it.

"We have to wedge the door shut!" shouted Julie.

Millie looked quickly around, then snatched up a long piece of nylon rope that was hung on the side of the wall within reach. She and Julie looped it around the door-knob three times, then Millie took the other end over to a steel bracing on the ship's side rail. Julie tied it securely.

Then Julie and Millie stepped back and looked at the bathroom door. The guard was shouting and pounding on the door, but the tightness of the rope would only allow the door to open about an inch.

"Now," said Julie, turning to Millie and taking the girl by the shoulders. "You said you were praying for the day when slavery was no more. And you said that was the only thing happening when suddenly you found yourself here."

"The boy," said Millie. She looked at Julie as if she just had just realized the answer. "The boy said the same thing!"

"What do you mean?"

"As he was preparing to take me on deck of the *Sallie M.* and I was praying aloud that slavery should be no more, the boy said almost the same thing. He said in a whisper, 'Slavery must end!' "

"What are you saying?"

"I think," said Millie, "that maybe the mind of the free and the mind of the slave, both thinking the same thing at the same time must have caused this to happen."

Julie's heart was pounding. Millie might be right. Both the boy and Millie, wanting the same thing at the same time, sent Millie forward into a time where slavery was no more. But why, she wondered, was there a switch? Why was Anne sucked back in time? Maybe it was like something she had studied in her eighth grade physical science class. She thought maybe the gap left by Millie demanded a replacement from the time into which she entered. This had drawn Anne back into that empty space.

It all made her head hurt. It made her soul ache.

"Millie," Julie said, "I think the only way I can get Anne back here to her time is for us to chant. We have to say over and over what you were saying when you came here. 'Slavery must be no more. Slavery must be no more.' But before we do I have to tell you I'm so glad I met you. And . . . I want to ask you if you would rather stay here and not go back. You and Anne are both my friends. To trade one for the other is a choice I can't make anymore. Earlier I thought I could make that choice. But not now." Julie felt tears in her eyes. She didn't try to wipe them away.

Millie gently put her good hand on Julie's arm. "I must go back," she said. "To me this is a nightmare. Nothing is familiar. Nothing makes any sense to me. I must be who I am and where I belong in time. Don't worry about me. I will be free. I am in Maryland now, the land that is the gateway to freedom in the North. I will be free, Julie. I will get away. Now that I've met you, I know it."

Julie barely nodded, tears rolling down her cheeks.

"And I have decided to change my name. No more slave name for me. Don't think of me as Millie anymore. I am naming myself Mariland, after the gateway. And my surname will be Rivers, for the waters that helped lead me to safety."

Julie's heart skipped a beat. She put her hand to her mouth and stared at Millie, at Mariland. She couldn't believe what she was hearing.

Mariland Rivers.

Mariland Rivers was the name of Julie's own great-great-great-great grandmother, who had indeed made it to freedom in New York and begun a family. Mariland Rivers's family moved to a small town west of Baltimore in the early 1900s and had lived there ever since.

"You," began Julie, hardly able to breathe, "you are . . ."

Mariland smiled. "I will be all right. Don't worry. I will make it to freedom."

"Yes," Julie said in a whisper. "I know you will! I know you will!"

Then Mariland began to chant, "Slavery must be no more! Slavery must be no more!"

Shaking, crying, and smiling, Julie also began to chant, "Slavery must be no more, slavery must be no more!"

Twenty-five

"You've got your sticks, now," said Randolph. "Let's have this wager done so we can get my runaways back!"

Anne sat on the deck next to the post where Charles was tied. In her hands she held nine small sticks that Randolph had found along the sandy soil by the harbor's edge.

Randolph stood over her. His sword had been dropped to the deck and forgotten for the moment, but his whip was back at his side, and he ran his hand around it in a threatening manner.

But Anne tried to keep her thoughts positive. Randolph wouldn't be using the sword on Charles's fingers again, because Anne's bet was going to work. It was such a simple thing, and she was going to win freedom for both herself and Charles.

"I'm going to make nine sticks into ten," she said. "And I won't break a one."

"Do it, then," said Randolph. "And be ready to help me catch my runaways, gypsy."

Slowly and carefully, Anne began to lay the sticks down on the deck. She lined some of them up side by side, some perpendicular to each other. When she was done, she sat back on her heels and smiled up at Randolph.

"There you go," she said. "I've made nine sticks into ten."

On the deck at her knees, the nine sticks had been used to form the letters of the word "TEN."

Charles looked down from the post and cried, "She did it!"

Randolph leaned over and put his hands on his thighs. He scowled at the sticks on the deck. In the lantern glow his eyes were mad, sparkling points of light. "There are still only nine!" he shouted. "What are you trying to tell me?"

"No," said Anne. "I made the bet and I won! See, the nine sticks spell 'ten.' "

"See," Charles agreed, "they *do* spell ten. She didn't say she would make ten sticks, she just said she would make ten out of nine sticks."

Randolph stood straight with a roar. "I don't read, you stupid gypsy! I never learned how to read and for all I know, you are telling me a lie!"

Anne felt her heart squeeze and her lungs freeze in her chest. The bet had failed.

"Not only did you lose your bet," Randolph shouted, "but you are lying to me as well! For that, you and Charles will receive beatings before we go after the runaways. Then, the two of you will die together!"

Anne was up in a flash, not even realizing what she was doing until she had snatched the sword from the deck and was holding it up in front of her. It was heavy and she needed both hands to hold it. Her arm muscles trembled, but she would not give in to them. "You aren't going to touch us!" she screamed. "This is all wrong, so wrong! You don't have the right to catch people who should be free, or beat people, or kill people!"

Randolph almost smiled. Slowly, he uncoiled his whip and pointed the handle at Anne. "You never saw me wager with my whip, did you, girl? You don't know how good I am at killing little insects who get in my way."

Then with a crack, Randolph snapped the whip in Charles's direction. The leather caught the boy around his ribs and he cried out in pain. When it pulled away, there was a vicious red mark on Charles's skin.

"I'm good with my whip," Randolph said. "And I bet you never handled a sword in your worthless life."

"Run now, Anne!" shouted Charles.

"I can't leave you like that!" Anne said.

The whip whistled in the air and caught Charles again. He groaned and cried, "Run away! Don't worry about me!"

Randolph laughed and coiled the whip again, ready to strike once more.

But in a lightning move, Anne lifted the sword, ran forward, and sliced the rope that held the boy to the post. Charles stumbled forward and fell to the deck.

"Get up, Charles!" Anne screamed.

Before Charles could gain his footing, the whip

lashed out again, this time in Anne's direction, wrapping around the blade of the sword and jerking it from her grasp. It flew in the night air and clattered to the deck too far away for her to get it without passing Randolph.

Randolph chuckled. With long strides, he walked around Anne and stood between her and her possible escape down the gangplank. He put one hand on his hip. The other hand held the whip. He made lazy figure eights in the air with the long leather lash.

Anne stared in horror. Charles, now standing, shook his head in resignation.

"Now," the man hissed, "now we'll have our punishment."

Twenty-six

Side by side on the downstairs passengers' deck of the double-decker tourist boat, Julie and Mariland chanted.

"Slavery must be no more, slavery must be no more, slavery must be no more."

They could hear the security guard and his dog inside the bathroom, still struggling to get out. The man was calling to them, pleading that he was going to lose his job if they didn't let him out at once. The dog, clearly confused, took turns barking, growling, and whining.

Julie's jaws were getting tired with the chant, but there was nothing else they could do. Soon, she hoped, someone on the same ship in 1849 would say something against slavery and bring Anne home again.

"Slavery must be no more, slavery must be no more."

Suddenly, there were bright, flashing lights shining on the tourist boat from the shore. Julie turned away from Mariland and looked out through the window.

There was a security car on the shore. The lights on the roof of the car were spinning, and its headlights were shining directly on the boat. Two guards had climbed out of the car and were coming, guns and flashlights in hand, down the pier to the plank.

One called out, "George, are you there? We got a message something was wrong. You'd called for help, then you didn't answer back."

Mariland stopped chanting. "Who are they?"

"They'll take us away if they catch us," Julie answered. Her blood pounded in her throat. "We can't let them catch us. We can't help Anne if they take us from the harbor."

Julie grabbed Mariland's hand and they ran to the railing on the other side of the boat. Below them, black water slapped against the boat sides.

"We have to jump," Julie said.

"I'm afraid," said Mariland.

"Trust me."

The flashlight beams were on the deck of the boat now. Footsteps walked around the side of the cabin, coming toward the girls.

"George," called one man. "Can you hear us? Where are you?"

"Now!" cried Julie.

"Slavery must be no more!" Mariland shouted.

The girls swung their legs over the railing of the boat.

Twenty-seven

"You can't get around him, Anne," said Charles. "Don't try. It will only be worse for you when he grabs you!"

Anne looked at Randolph, who stood grinning his insane grin. She looked over at Charles, who stood in fear of the fate that was his. She looked behind her at the side of the *Sallie M.* that faced the open water of the Patapsco River.

"No matter what happens," Anne said to Charles, "remember, we set a lot of people free. Never forget that."

"I won't," Charles said. "It's something I'll be proud of all my life, even if my life is only a few more hours long."

"Stop chattering," Randolph said. "Come to me and I'll tie you together. Then we'll all roam the streets and find those escaped slaves. My time is running out! My gold is on the line!" He snapped the whip to stress his command.

"You told me you can't swim," Anne whispered to Charles. "I can. Do you want to try with me?"

"Be quiet!" Randolph shouted. "Come over here.

Now!" The man stepped forward and both Anne and Charles backed up.

"Do you want to try?" Anne shouted to Charles.

Charles stared at Randolph, approaching with his whip, snarling like a mad dog who had trapped a raccoon. Charles glanced over his shoulder at the dark water of the harbor. Suddenly, he grabbed Anne's hand.

"Yes!" he cried.

The two jumped over the side of the ship and fell toward the water. Air rushed around Anne's ears, making them sting.

As he fell, Charles shouted, "Slavery must die!"

Twenty-eight

Julie hit the cold water with Mariland's cry to her side. "Slavery must be no more!"

Anne hit the cold water with Charles's cry to her side. "Slavery must die!"

Twenty-nine

It seemed like a long time before the water slowed her down and she was able to begin working one arm to bring her back up to the surface. The *Sallie M.* was a tall ship, and the long fall had driven the two of them deep into the water, so deep Anne was surprised her feet hadn't touched bottom. She couldn't see Charles but she felt the hand still in hers, trusting her, praying, she was sure, that she would bring him up to air and then help him swim to shore far enough away that Randolph couldn't find them.

Her free arm worked against the water. Out, around, down, out, around, down, pulling the two up. Her lungs were already aching with the need for oxygen. The hand in hers held tightly. She knew Charles was struggling for breath, too, but he wasn't fighting her.

And then her fingertips broke the surface, and then her face and she gasped. Air rushed into her lungs, sweet night air. Her eyes opened, and she saw stars in the sky and a chalk-dot moon hanging over the roof of the National Aquarium.

The aquarium? she thought. *The aquarium?*

The person beside her, still holding her hand, broke the surface and took a loud, raspy breath of air.

Anne turned her head and looked.

Julie was beside her in the water, her eyes wide, her mouth open in a smile of wonder.

"Anne!" Julie cried.

"Julie!"

Laughing and crying at the same time, they paddled ashore and with effort climbed the log wall to the sandy ground above. There they sat, shivering and trembling in wet clothes, staring at each other. They were too happy and too tired to speak.

A flashlight shone over on them from the pier of the tourist boat. It was a security guard.

"What are you girls doing there?" the man called. "Don't you know there's no swimming allowed in the harbor? You could have been hit by a boat, or worse."

Anne coughed, then called back, "I'm sorry. We won't do it again, we promise."

"We promise," Julie added.

"All right, then," said the guard. He flicked off the light and went to his car. The second man stepped off the gangplank onto the pier, leading the security guard and dog that Mariland and Julie had trapped in the bathroom.

"They ran away, I'm sure," the guard was saying. "One of the girls was wearing a funny costume. I'll never forget her. The other one, though, she looked like every other young teenage girl."

The two officers climbed into the car and pulled

away, joking from their open window that maybe the first guard shouldn't underestimate teenage girls. As his friends drove off, the guard with the dog glanced over at Anne and Julie, frowned for a moment, then walked away.

"He only remembered Millie," Julie said.

"What?" asked Anne.

"He only remembered Millie. I mean Mariland," Julie repeated. "And she's going to be free, Anne! I know it!"

Anne wrapped her fingers around her knees and looked up at the bright lights of Baltimore's Inner Harbor. "I hope Charles will be free," she said. "But I guess I'll never know."

"Charles?"

"I want to believe he made it."

"I don't know who he is," Julie said, "but if you believe it, it could happen."

Wearily, Anne nodded.

The two girls sat in silence for a while, then they got up, shook themselves off, and went to find a phone so they could call their parents.

Books used as reference in writing *Maryland: Ghost Harbor*—

Enchantment of America: Maryland by Allan Carpenter; 1966, Children's Press, Chicago, IL.

Historic Baltimore by Priscilla L. Miles; 1987, Priscilla Miles, Baltimore, MD.

Legends, Lies, and Cherished Myths of American History by Richard Shenkman; 1988, William Morrow and Co., New York, NY.

Maryland in Words and Pictures by Dennis Fradin; 1980, Children's Press, Chicago, IL.

The Underground Railroad by Charles L. Blockson; 1987, Prentice Hall, New York, NY.

The World Book Encyclopedia, Volume 13; 1986, World Book, Inc., Chicago, IL.

If you'd like to read more about Maryland or the Underground Railroad—

Maryland in Words and Pictures by Dennis Fradin; 1980, Children's Press, Chicago, IL.

. . . If You Traveled on the Underground Railroad by Ellen Levine; 1992, Scholastic Inc., New York, NY.

The Maryland Colony by Dennis Fradin; 1990, Children's Press, Chicago, IL.

Stuck on the USA; 1994, Gosset and Dunlap, New York, NY.

Rand McNally Children's Atlas of the United States; 1994, Rand McNally and Company.

Fabulous Facts About the 50 States by Wilma S. Ross; 1991, Scholastic Inc., New York, NY.